THEIR BACKS
AGAINST THE WALL

THEIR BACKS AGAINST THE WALL

Love, Money and Life

Terence Merritt

iUniverse, Inc.
Bloomington

Their Backs against the Wall
Love, Money, and Life

This is a work of fiction. All of the characters, names, incidents, organizations, and dialogue in this novel are either the products of the author's imagination or are used fictitiously.

iUniverse books may be ordered through booksellers or by contacting:

iUniverse
1663 Liberty Drive
Bloomington, IN 47403
www.iuniverse.com
1-800-Authors (1-800-288-4677)

ISBN: 978-1-4620-4357-6 (sc)
ISBN: 978-1-4620-4356-9 (hc)
ISBN: 978-1-4620-4374-3 (ebk)

Printed in the United States of America

iUniverse rev. date: 08/11/2011

Those who hate me
Shall hate me

Those who love me
Have loved me

Those who know me
Still know me

Chapter One

The Beginning

I knew this day would come. I knew that, one day, this could happen to me. You may think it only happens in the movies. But it actually happened to me. I was getting married to the one woman who made me feel and see things clearly. She made me feel better about myself and my life choices. Karen was my seventh rib, and I needed her always by my side. Thank you, God!

I always asked myself how and when it started. After all, love wasn't just something you hoped for; it was something you would die for. I could see the day Karen and I met clearly. It had been cold, and Chicago had been just as beautiful as it had always been.

But standing here in the church made that day seem dreamlike. As I looked around, I could only thank God that I'd met Karen. *Man, I tell you, look at David, Lay, Kelano, Al, and my man, Jesus—all dressed up and finally got a place to go.* I chuckled inwardly. Sam looked mad as hell. Sam—Samantha Wright—was one of my past lovers. She asked me last night if she could come to the rehearsal, and I asked Karen. That did not go over very well at first, but Karen said she wanted to keep an eye on Sam while I was at my bachelor party. Given the time Sam put in on me, I was surprised she'd come. She had been very close to me, and she'd asked me to marry her. After that, I'd decided to never again date a girl I worked with.

Today was not my day; it was hers—my baby, Karen's. I watched Karen walk toward me down the aisle. "Ribbon in the Sky" played at a low level, and everyone was chitchatting and having fun. It was such a good feeling to be here at this moment of my life. All I could say was, *Hell yeah.* Sometimes I liked to sit back and remember just how this relationship started and how we'd gotten here. I had been a part of a lot of bad relationships and knew that God had finally brought me my life partner and my best friend. I'd had a lot of growing up to do before he had. I do remember how it started, and I do know now that I would not have it any other way.

I had just moved to Chicago—well I'd been there around eight or nine months. It was a typical, cold day in November. The temperature was about 35 degrees, and it was very sunny. As I walked out of the building, I looked over my head. I could see the iron rails and the train rolling across above. It was the red line. This was one of the four color-coded rail lines that transported the people of Chicago. The line ran from the suburbs to the inner city.

Skyscrapers stood on all four corners. I was dressed in dark blue Tommy slacks with the cuff reaching the third eyelid of my Stacy Adams and a white, long-sleeve FUBU shirt hanging out of my pants. I worked on computers. All day, I either answered questions on the phone or gave hands-on training to personnel in my department. I mean this job was gravy, and I did not want to lose it or change jobs—not in the near future, at any rate. All around me, people ran around, mad about being cold or mad about nothing at all.

It was lunchtime. My office was on the corners of Adams and Wells. I crossed to get lunch, and as I did, I saw the meals-on-wheels truck—not the one that gave assistance to the poor, but the one that sold soul food and island food at lunch and sometimes late at night downtown. This heavy food was not on my mind for lunch today. I needed my fix. So I went across the street to McDonald's.

Chicago seemed so far away from home. I didn't mind because I'd always traveled, ever since I was a kid. I'd moved from the burrows of New York City to the country of Savannah, Georgia. Where I was didn't make a difference to me. I'd traveled around the world and some places twice. I was going to make wherever I laid my hat a home.

"Can I help you?" the young girl behind the counter asked. She couldn't have been more then eighteen or nineteen years old. I immediately thought of R. Kelly, and I laughed inside. I knew that this girl wasn't fourteen or anything like that, but she did look that young. I wondered whether she was in college and living at home with parents. *Perhaps I shouldn't be so stereotypical*, I thought. Being a black person, I tended to think I could read other people, and most of the time, I was all wrong. Yeah, all black people think we're psychics.

At any rate, I continued to think about this young, pretty girl as she made orders for the millions. Was she a parent? Was she a single mother? Was this her only means of income? I thought of this only because she looked good in the normal drab of a Mickey-D's uniform. And I was considering being flirty, so I could get her phone number. "Yes, let me have a six-piece nugget and small fries with a medium coke," I finally dragged out of my mouth.

"A number five combo," she said. "Would you like to supersize that?"

"No thank you," I said.

As I backed away from the counter, I heard, "That's not much for a big man like you." I heard the words, but I didn't think they were directed toward me.

I turned around, not expecting to see what I saw. The voice came from the most beautiful, caramel-colored woman I'd seen in some time. She was about four eleven with light brown hair that was long and beautiful. In that moment, I only knew that she was lovely, and her beauty left me in shock for a minute—not a second but a whole minute; I needed that whole minute to absorb her beauty. *Why she is pushing up on me?* I was thinking. She reminded me of another woman from my past, but that woman was totally different. The woman from my past had taken my heart and broken it twice. I didn't plan to let that happen again. You see, I was about six one, and I weighed about 240 pounds. I was a good size, and people respected that.

But I responded to this beauty standing behind me. "Negative," I stated quickly, without thinking. "It's just what I need," I added, with the normal confidence with which I carried myself. I could not believe that I'd said negative. That was one of my many clichés that I used. The military was still ingrained in my mind, and I couldn't help how I responded sometimes. To be honest, she was lucky though. I didn't say, "Negative, cat woman," like I normally do when I disagree with a lady or young girl.

All this confidence came from six years that I'd spent in the army—infantry. Man, I'd run through a lot of women when I was in the military! I'd been in Germany twice, Korea, Japan, Italy, and Greece. While in Greece, I had island-hopped for a week aboard a yacht, *London.*

For a moment, I was lost in memory, but I quickly brought myself back to this beauty in front of me.

"Oh yeah," the young lady stated, now standing beside me.

I could tell she'd moved to get a better look at me.

"I see. It all settles right there!" She pointed at my stomach and pushed it in a little.

I giggled a little like the Pillsbury doughboy.

5

We laughed.

I had expanded after the military and wished that I hadn't. But if you loved me, you loved me. If you didn't, you didn't have to. I was good with mine.

"Ha, ha, you got jokes," she said.

I quickly put out my hand. "My name is Jerry, the comedian. And who are you?" I asked the question like I was introducing her on stage.

"My name is Karen—Karen Watson." Karen wore a knee-high skirt that was made from a Liz Claiborne collection with Prada boots, and she carried a handbag from D&G. Her blouse was sheer and in good taste; I saw the slight hint of cleavage. She wore a sweater that hung over her shoulders.

I then give her my complete name. "Jerry G. Jones."

She turned away to make her order. Once she was finished, she looked back to find me. As Karen walked over, she said, "You mean like the owner of the Dallas Cowboys?"

I was shocked that she even knew who the Cowboys owner was; also I hadn't thought that she would come over to me again. That was why I'd moved away—to see if she would move toward me. And now I knew that she knew football. I wondered if she liked basketball and baseball too. As we were living in Chicago, there was a good chance that she did. I had always wanted to meet a woman who could go to a game with me and didn't just act like she knew what she was looking at.

"Sir, sir." I finally heard the young lady from the counter who I'd been checking out minutes ago. "Here is your order, sir."

"You're not eating here?" Karen asked.

"Well I wasn't, but it would be nice to have some company for lunch today," I replied.

The young girl at the counter called Karen to retrieve her bag, and we took a booth looking out onto Adams Street.

"Well," she asked again, "like Jerry Jones?"

"Yes, just like him. Where do you work?" I asked. *Damn, you know better than to ask a woman where she works. She might think you're a stalker. It's like asking her her age. Dumb move!*

But the question didn't seem to bother her too much. "I work right there." She pointed to the same building in which I worked. "On the seventh floor."

"Oh!" I said.

"And you?" she asked.

I was thinking that she would trip on the fact that we worked in the same place, but she didn't. "I work right there." I pointed at the same building. "But I'm on the third floor."

During lunch, we engaged in small talk—the get-to-know-you chat. I had confidence, or should I say swag. But there was something about this woman. She was so damn beautiful. I didn't want to say the wrong thing—you know, put my foot in my mouth. One thing I could say about me was that I carried myself like an alpha male. An alpha male is a man who is not weak and who is in control of his mind, body, and soul. The first time I heard the words *alpha male* was from a woman who was letting her boyfriend know why she was leaving him. I'd thought, *Damn, she's cold as hell.* But I could relate to what she was saying. She was leaving her man for me.

I hadn't known I was an alpha male until then. I was just glad I'd found that out at a young age.

"So, Jerry Jones, do you like football like your namesake?" Karen asked.

"Yes I do, and you?"

"Yes I do," she stated.

I joked. "Did we just get married?" *Damn, that was corny*, I thought.

She laughed, and that made me feel more comfortable. A man cannot have a really good conversation with a woman he's interested in unless he's comfortable, and Karen seemed to know how to make me feel that way. She made sure to talk and keep that annoying silence monster at bay. We laughed and decided that we'd taken too long at lunch.

As we walked out to the street, Karen spoke to me, and I paid attention to every word that came out of her mouth. I felt that she meant everything she said. I looked deep into her eyes and could see she enjoyed life and enjoyed her job. It seemed that we walked a long way, but we'd just crossed the street. I believed in listening to what women had to say because I believed in love. Corny again, but if I didn't listen to this woman, someone else would. She spoke clearly and with a touch of sex appeal. I felt like she and I were the only two people on the street. Nothing other than us mattered at that moment. Those crystal brown eyes looked so loving. I searched to make sure they were the real deal, and they were. I couldn't help but compare her to Damon Dash's cousin, Stacey Dash.

Karen looked at me and asked, "Do you want to know?" as if she could read my mind. She looked into my eyes and replied, "Yes, they're real, and they are all mine." As she said this, she slicked her lips and laughed softly, as if to hint she was all woman. She thought I was looking at her lips, when I was lost in her eyes.

At the end of the conversation, we decided to exchange phone numbers and to call each other after work. As we went upstairs Karen looked into my eyes again. "You'd better call me after work."

"Now, you know I will," I said.

With a smile, I shook her hand and exited the elevator on the third floor. As I went back to work, I tried not to make much of this meeting. But I kept thinking of Karen. Her body was made from the finest ingredients. Her behind was a nice one; it stood up and was round like a perfect basketball. Her legs were thick but not too thick. They were the legs of a runner. I could tell she ran. Her eyes were like two light brown jewels. *I could get lost in her eyes all the time*, I thought to myself.

Damn, I reminded myself, I had not come here to Chicago to fall in love or to meet somebody. And I damn well didn't want to meet someone who worked in the same building I worked in. I had come here to start new, to leave my past life behind me. There was much more I wanted to do. I had left my money and bad life behind me. I wanted to be an average Joe. That did not mean getting hitched like Will Smith. I did want to be in a real relationship—to have only one love. But this was too soon. Why was I thinking so far ahead? I hadn't even been on the first date with this woman. I hadn't even been here for a full year, and I didn't like knowing too many people at the job or where I lived.

I went back to working in my cubicle. I thought of Karen and how good she smelled. I liked her hair and her way of speaking. Meeting Karen had made me feel a little light-headed. She was the first person I'd met who I wanted to see outside of work. I kept to myself. I had been around some of the richest and the poorest people in the world. And I'd found out they were all the same. The similarity had nothing to do with wealth or appearance but with attitude. You could go anywhere in this world and find the same people wherever you went. This was why I expected the worst out of everyone I met. I knew that sooner or later, people would say something wrong out of their dumb ass mouths. Sometimes they said things to hurt you, and sometimes they just said dumb stuff to get under your skin. And if they aimed to hurt you, it was because jealously had touched their minds and hearts.

Then I thought about the woman Karen reminded me of—Marissa! I did not want to think about this woman, but your mind could take you places sometimes even when you didn't care to remember. This woman had made my heart feel like it had been removed with a dirty spoon. With her, I had gone against my own rules—you never go back to a person when he or she leaves you for another person. Like a dumb ass, I had done so. I had done so, and I had paid for my decision with heartbreak. I had given that woman everything. That was my problem. As my mother would say, "Jerry, you give so much of yourself to those women. That means you're no damn good. They use you and abuse you. That's what they do." It seemed

Mom always had a song to go along with her speeches. And it seemed that Mom was always right about me.

My mother was a loving, Red Bone woman who had become a grandmother overnight. Her first grandchild had come along when she was about fifty. But before she could take notice, she had two grandsons and had gained about a hundred pounds on her once small frame.

I had never spent that much time with my mother. She was there on the phone, but for the most part, my grandparents had raised me. I loved my mother though—dearly.

As time went on, my relationship with Karen grew. We became closer than close. Our conversations were about life, us, Chicago, and our goals together and as individuals. Months ago, things had seemed to be so bleak and dim for me. Now I was in Chi-town and loving the cold weather, food, and my place in this world. You see, I'd chosen to move here because I'd wanted an easy job where no one could bother me. My life in the past had been very lonely, and money-hungry people had seemed to have had a blue crab's hold on me. I hadn't been without a woman or so-called friends, but I'd still been alone. And I could go back to it if only I made one phone call.

But for now, this was where I wanted to be—to be a nobody for awhile, to be Jerry again! I wanted to be under the radar, and I have to tell you, it felt good.

My brother, David, tapped me on the sleeve. I guess he must have seen me and wondered what I was looking at. "Jay, you need to be paying attention to your girl. She sees you looking over there."

My gaze had drifted over the heads of the people in the church, but now my attention was back on Karen and her light brown eyes. As her father walked up, he gave me a look that told me he was proud to hand her over to me. Her father and mother were the coolest people I had met in a long while.

They had not been cool when Karen and I were first living together, but since we'd decided to get hitched, they had seemed to come around. Her parents had said something once to both of us about shacking up. Then they'd let it go.

Karen's father's name was Henry M. Watson, and her mother was Barbara A. Watson. Karen had two older sisters named Alicia and Renee. Both were fine as hell like Karen. But Renee was a special case—the kind of woman who wanted all the attention—and she was mad as hell that her younger sister had found true love before she had.

They were all living with their parents—all three of them! I recall a time on the Fourth of July when I went into the house to use the restroom, and Renee was sitting on the commode. As I opened the door, I felt badly and quickly turned to exit. Renee called out to me, and I answered through the door.

"You can come in and help me clean myself up," she said.

I just walked away and never told Karen about the incident.

I liked to see single women staying with their mother and father. It gave them a sense of innocence—well it did for all but one in that house. Karen and her sisters were all Daddy's little girls.

Karen's sister, Alicia, was the other good girl in the house—or so I once thought. Alicia was very tall and had a beautiful, dark skin tone. One trait the family shared was their hair. Barbara never had the girl's hair cut, so each one of then looked like they were ready to be a model. Alicia had the longest hair of the three. She had legs that made a man say, "I want to know you." And she liked it when they said it. Her breasts were young and perky, and she had lips to match. The one thing I really liked about her was the outfits she wore. They were classy but had a hint of freaky slut in them. She had no problem showing the world her body parts. Alicia had a freaky side that showed every time she was out and about. I'd caught her in the club giving her man more than a little bit. I once found her and him in her father's backyard almost butt booty naked. I really thought that Renee was bad, but Alicia took the cake. She was a gold digger and told everyone that she was. But, I guess she backed it up well enough because the rich guys did not mind paying for what she asked for. I guess that Alicia and her man must have needed some sex really bad for that type of action.

I sometimes asked Karen who had taught who—her or Alicia. Or was it a family trait? Then I would laugh, and Karen would get a little upset with me. Ever since Karen learned that I'd seen one of her sisters half naked and the other giving more than a little to guys, Karen kept a close eye on her sisters when they were around me.

It's amazing what you can think about in a split second. I turned to face the preacher. Then I smiled, looking over at Alicia and Renee. If they only knew what I was thinking! Wow.

Standing at that altar made me feel sleepy and bored. *Damn how much longer?* I wondered. I was getting ready to leave. Karen knew how my mind wandered. I thought it was some type of disorder or something. I daydreamed about my past a lot. But my past was just that—my past. Karen was the future and I will make our future the best she had ever dreamed of. I believed that God put people into people's lives for a reason, a season, or a lifetime. And I was going to keep Karen with me for a lifetime. With Karen by my side, we now faced forward. I whispered to Karen, "I promise you, darling, you will have your Cinderella story."

She gave my hand a great squeeze and smiled up at me. She whispered to me that I was her ribbon in the sky.

I smiled, she smiled, and her father winked at me.

Karen deserved to be happy. She had gone through a lot. I was going to be the man I knew she wanted. I would wait on her, bring her breakfast in bed, listen to her, buy her gifts just because, and love her and only her unconditionally—all day and every day. This was my vow to her. This was my wife and my life. I really truly loved her. But when I got in the limo after the wedding, she was going to get all of big daddy. I laughed inside and winked back at her father. If he only knew what I was thinking.

There I went—my 89 percent. Men think about sex 89 percent of the time, and we cannot help it. But I was in a church, and I needed to stop thinking about sex. That was not what this relationship was built on.

As I looked at Karen, I realized that not all her bridesmaids were here. We were short one. I could hear my mother and Mrs. Watson wanting to start the rehearsal over again, and I sighed.

David patted me on the back and said, "Can we go outside and get a smoke break? I cannot do this back to back again."

"Yeah, this is the third time, bro," Lay said. "Let's go."

"Hey, everyone," I yelled. "Let's take a ten-minute break so Karen can talk things over with her mother and my mother." I looked down at Karen. "Baby, I will be outside okay?"

"Jerry, don't take long," she replied. "I want to get this done and over with too."

"I'll be right outside," I assured her. "When you need me, tell me. I will come running!"

We let go of each other's hands. The guys and I walked down the aisle to the doors leading outside. Kelano said he would stay in. Being from the islands, he did not like the cold.

"Damn, it's cold out here," Lay said.

"Man, you in front of the church," I said. "Mind your mouth."

"My fault, dog, but it is cold as hell."

"Hell is not cold," David retorted.

"How you know, David? You were there?"

"Stop calling me David, man," David complained. "Call me Dee at least, man!"

"You two stop the fussing," I cut in. "Let's move away from the door."

"Man, how is Karen these days?" Lay asked me.

"What is your problem? Why you bring that up?" David said defensively.

"Dee, it's okay," I said softly. "She good." I pulled on the cigarette and thought back to that day when we first thought that might not be the case.

It was about four months into our relationship when Karen called me at work after an appointment with her doctor. She had told me that she had a doctor's appointment that day. She sounded so sad over the phone. She said, "Jerry, when you get off work, I need to talk to you—you know, as a man. I started thinking of what I had done wrong.

Karen had called me around one, and I didn't get off until four. As I pulled up to my place, she was already there. I just knew I had done something. As I reached for my things from the car, she was walking up to me with tears in her eyes.

"Baby, what's wrong?" I asked with the concern of a father seeing his little girl's eyes running with tears.

"Let's go inside."

I placed all my objects by the front door. As we walked to the sofa, she turned and broke down in a loud cry. "They said," she paused, "they said I have breast cancer."

Her words were so mumbled together I asked her to repeat herself. "Karen, I can't understand what you said," I whispered. "Baby, what's going on?"

She repeated the diagnosis. I looked at her and words—the English language—were lost to my mind. I could not think, move, or react.

I didn't know what to say. I just stood there and pulled her close and held her as I once had—on the day when I told her that I loved her for the first time. Years ago, I would not have given a woman a chance with crying on me. But I had changed, and I wanted love. The love that we shared was so true, and I sometimes felt that I lived a life like in the movie *The Best Man*—you know a life with good job, a great income, your own place, a beautiful woman by your side, and the car of your dreams—oh yeah, and your Rottweiler. I was too upset to think I was living a good life now. I only wanted the hurt to stop.

I led Karen to the sofa to sit. As she explained what her doctor had told her, I could only reply with tears of my own. Dr. Henrique had told her that she had breast cancer. And the only reason he had found out so soon was because the breast exam she had taken had revealed a node in her chest. "That was why I had to go in for that mammogram," Karen explained. Normally women didn't have mammograms until they were in their forties. "This node was too large to go unnoticed," she added.

That day we sat and held each other.

Karen came around about thirty minutes later to ask me if I was going to leave her.

"Why would you say that?" I asked.

"I may lose one of my breasts," she replied.

I looked into her eyes and, never looking away, said, "I don't care. If that is the case, I will be by your side anyway. I love you, baby, and nothing is going to change that."

I was now hearing my mentor, leader, and father figure—my grandfather. My grandfather was a great man! That man had been done over, done to, and just plain old done. But he still fought back every day, every year, and every time. I never have seen him make excuses. He took whatever life threw at him like a man and was the first man I knew who always loved me. As I grew to manhood, I watched him, and he taught me that a true man loves and respects his mate. He was the true meaning of an alpha male.

I tried over and over again to live by his standards, and nine times out of ten, I did. I had made a lot of mistakes and bad judgment calls. But that was all in growing up. There was one thing I knew, though. He had said to me one day while sitting under his carport, "You always love your mate, your woman, and your wife."

To me Karen was two out of the three, and I was not going to leave her when times got rough—at least not like Marissa had done me. The truth when it came to love was not difficult. And Karen and I had true love. I knew that at this point we had only been together for about four months, but there had come a time when she proved that she would be there for me, and I had done the same for her. This was just another test—for our love for each other.

I told Karen that we had been together this long and had passed other tests and that we would pass this. "Okay," I said, pulling her close and wiping the tears from her eyes. I reached over to her soft, wet face. "You are the water that flows over my rocky life and makes it smooth." This was a quote that I had said to her on special occasions. But I now said it to reassure her that I loved her and would be there through the test of time. "Baby," I continued, "God has given me a flower, and with this flower I shall grow."

"You are my rock that holds my dam together so that it don't overflow," Karen replied.

Then we kissed, and I said that I loved her very much.

"I love you more," she answered.

"We will take life back into our hands, baby," I told her.

Some people did not believe in love, and I was one of them. It seemed as if *love* was a word used like sex. It was good when you used it, and after that, it was over. You never minded not using it again for a while.

"I have to be seen by another doctor next week, on Friday. He will tell me how serious this is and whether I need surgery or if there is no hope," Karen said.

"I'll go with you when you go back to see him," I told her. "And let's take tomorrow off. Let's just enjoy the day. I mean, it's Friday, and I know I can. Can you?" I asked.

"Yes, my supervisor said I could have it off anyway because of this. Did you wash clothes this week yet?" Karen asked.

"Yeah, they're in the basement."

"Is my muumuu clean?" Karen asked with a smile of comfort and love.

"Yes, it's in your dresser drawer."

That night, we watched all her favorite shows and rented *Legends of the Fall*. Karen had a thing for Brad Pitt. It seemed it was okay for a black woman to say a white man was fine as hell. But let a brother say that about a fine ass white woman. He would get his head knocked the hell off. Anyway, Karen loved that movie. After Chinese food and good entertainment, we went to the bedroom to retire for the night. As usual, she went into the bathroom first and brushed her teeth, and then I used the bathroom. As we cuddled, Karen asked me to make love to her.

So I did.

I reached for the remote to the stereo and pressed play. I had Syleena Johnson, an artist from Chicago, in the CD player, and "Tonight I'm Gonna Let Go" was playing in seconds. I dimmed the lights so that we could see a little more than shadows. As I straddled her, I notice that she hadn't any panties on. So I gave her what she liked the most. I pulled the light blue and pink muumuu over her head. As I did, her long hair fell almost perfectly back in order. Was I tripping or was it true that Karen had never looked more beautiful. Even at her worst I felt she was beautiful. I reached to pull the hair out of her eyes as she laid back.

She welcomed me with her arms open and said, "Come here, Daddy."

I began to kiss her on her small but strong shoulders, remembering all the time that my baby worked out three times a week. While moving very slowly south, I reached the top of her breast and made a circle around her nipple, making sure not to touch them. Being a reader of all types of books from doctors, lawyers, and life gurus has taught me more than the average person knows. I read that the nipple is a women's center of pleasure, so a man should always try not to go straight to them. And given the current situation I wanted to show her that a breast or nipple did not make a woman; she did. I licked and sucked on the top and bottom of both of her breasts, while my right hand grabbed her ass cheek and massaged it over and over. Karen's ass was not too soft and never too hard.

Karen felt overheated and had a pre-orgasm while I was fingering her and sucking on her breast. Not even when she reached her climax did Karen lose control. She made a pleasurable sound that assured me that she was happy and feeling good. I then softly bit her left nipple and with a quick suckle, she seemed to have another semi-organism again. I reached back with my left hand and placed two more fingers in her womb.

She whispered, "I love you, Jerry."

I replied back with a mouthful of breast, "I love you too, Karen."

As a growing young man, I had learned that you better call a woman's name at least two to three times while having sex with her, to let her know that you are not thinking of someone else. I had to laugh inside because I did that once—called a girl the wrong name. But here and now it was all about pleasing Karen. Karen's body shook and my fingers were as wet as the water that flows over a rapid, full, rocky river. I watched her body move up and down as I kept felling deeper into her lovely womanhood. Karen could not take it anymore, and she tried to place me inside her. I pulled back, and she looked puzzled. I then rolled her onto her stomach and started to lick and suck my way down to her ass. As I kissed her ass, I told her she could never tell me to kiss her ass because I would reply that I already had. We both laughed a little.

I then rolled her back over. I parted her walls of brown and pink love. Juices flowed down her thigh, and I could only say to myself, *Damn, she is fine.* As I bent down, I could see her clitoris. Then I slipped the tip of my tongue across it. Karen's legs became tense and shook some more. I placed her legs on my shoulders and buried my face between her legs. She tasted so good, so sweet. I was nearing the point of placing myself inside her. But I had a rule. She had to come first, and I would come last. I believed that the women should receive at least two organisms in one session. So, I kept my tongue at work and held her legs on top of my shoulders until her hips leaped off the bed and she held my head tightly against her soft walls. Yes, I could hardly breathe. But I was a big boy, and I could take it. And take it I did, all over my face.

As I slid inside Karen, I wiped my mouth and eased in slowly. She placed her nails deep in my back. Sweat was dripping off of both of us. Karen pulled me down harder, so that all ten inches of me was deeper inside her then earlier. I felt that spot we all have felt before. I felt the end of her womanhood and she screamed in pain and pleasure. As she screamed, she came again, and all hell broke loose between her legs.

The bed under her was soaked and slippery. I pulled back for one deep push and stayed in deep. I felt her back. As she pounded over and over, the air had gotten thick with passion, sweat, heat. Our bodies moved in tighter in rhythm with each other. I felt my penis starting to throb. I felt like I was going to break her in two.

I pinned down her legs forward, moving harder, deeper, stronger with every motion. Karen's nails were deep in my back, and she screamed again. I roared like a lion in the jungle on top of one of his female mates. We both collapsed beside each other with sweat pouring and love in our hearts. We held each other, said good night and I love you, and fell fast asleep.

Karen was doing fine. The surgery went well, and now she was here with me today.

"What is up with Sam?" Lay asked. "I see her in the church. She keeps moving her lips and trying to get your attention. If this woman tries something, I will . . . I don't know, but it will be ugly."

David and I laughed. That Lay was something. I took it he really liked Karen.

After we had our Newports, we went back in out of the cold air.

"I then say to you, Karen . . ." *Blah, blah, and blah.* Reverend Jesse Coles was addressing Karen, and when he'd come to an end, he asked, "And you say?"

"I will," she replied.

Next, the revered turned to me. "Then, Jerry, I say . . ." *Blah, blah, and blah*, was all I heard again until he asked, "And you say?"

"No!"

Karen and her parents all looked up at me in shock.

I quickly said, "I was just kidding! I'm just kidding. It's practice, baby. I will say, 'I will,' too."

"Jerry, just say I do, okay, and stop messing around," my mother told me.

As Karen looked up into my eyes, I could tell that she felt that no one—nothing—would stand in our way. "Okay, everyone, that's a wrap! Jerry, get my coat please, baby."

"Yeah, you don't have to go home, but ya gotta leave here," I heard a voice say from the back of the church.

As everyone in the church gathered his or her things and began to exit, I asked that we all stay and say a pray so that God would protect us as we left the church and rejoined each other tomorrow. Everyone chitchatted after the prayer. Karen and I waited by the front door. We shook hands and thanked everyone for being there tonight. And of course, Karen reminded those with specific jobs to be on time. I immediately grabbed her hand to guide her outside. I wanted to be next to her, to hold her before we departed.

The wind coming off Lake Michigan made the air feel fresh. Karen and I both loved the winter chill. We hugged, and as I danced along the sidewalk, I said, "I'm going to get my freak on."

I started to run a little, and Karen caught up to me. She hit me across the head lightly and jumped up on me. The night air was cutting into my face and the skyline was clear. The stars were out and bright, and I felt that nothing could go wrong. I let Karen down after a quick kiss. I looked away to reply to something my father had said, but Karen turned me so that I faced her. We looked into each other's eyes and gave each other a long, loving kiss. We heard our friends and family making comments like, "Get a room," "Ahhh," "That is so cute," and, "They look good together."

"Jerry, what are you going to do tonight?"

"I told you," I replied. "I am going to get my freak on!"

She repeated the question. I acted like I had not heard her. When I acted as if I was going to let go of her hand, she pulled me back. "Jerry, what are you going to do tonight?" she demanded.

"I am going to be a good boy for you," I told her.

"Not too much drinking and definitely no driving for you," she said with a cautioning tone.

"Okay, baby, okay!" I replied. "I got you. You always say I got you. And do I?"

"Yes, you do." She met my gaze. "I love you, and I just want everything to go right." It seemed as if she might start to cry.

"It will, Karen, everything will go as planned," I assured her, adding gently, "It's time for me to leave."

"Okay, Jerry," she said softly.

As the cars and taxis flew by in the windy city of downtown Chicago, I knew that Karen was not happy about me going to the bachelor's party. But, hell, she was having her own party too. As we walked down the sidewalk, we could see people having a good time, talking and planning for tonight and tomorrow. With a wave of my hand, I directed my brother to get the boys together and retrieve all of our cars.

I wrapped Karen up tight in her heavy DKNY coat and fastened the top button. "You stay warm and sweet," I told her. "I don't want to spend my entire time trying to thaw you out tomorrow night." I smiled and kissed her on her forehead. Karen liked when I did that. I'd found that a woman liked it when her man showed her attention and affection. It made her feel very special."

I was about to walk away when I heard a cry from the darkness. "Girlfriends!" Then it came again: "Girlfriends!" It was Anna, Karen's friend who lived in Japan somewhere and worked as a vice president of marketing. Anna James-Rinehart was a big-breasted, five feet nothing beauty. She walked like money, screamed like a white girl, and dressed like a millionaire. As Anna moved into the light, I could see the she loved to put on a lot of makeup. Her eye shadow was heavy, and her lipstick was painted on just like her foundation. You could see her beauty, but she covered it with makeup. Given what I'd gleaned about her from the phone conversations she and Karen had, I didn't like her. But Karen assured me that Anna was a sweet girl.

As I stepped away to give Karen room, she pulled me back. "Stay," she said, like I was some kind of dog.

"Yes, master," I replied.

Karen gave me a nasty look that said, *You know what I mean.* Then she introduced me to Anna. I knew I still wouldn't like this girl. She smelled of trouble. They say that women have a sixth sense. Well men have a dumb girlfriend sense.

"Hey, girl," Karen greeted. Then she looked at me. "Anna, this is my man—my soon-to-be husband—Jerry."

"Hello," Anna said.

"Baby, this is my girl, Anna."

"What's up?" I replied, my tone a little sharp and grim.

We shook hands.

Anna dressed like she talked—sharp and with a lot of attitude! You could tell she wasn't just about money; she was made from it. But my lady had told me the truth about her. Anna had grown up with money, but as a girl she'd always wanted to be a hood rat. In high school, she got her butt whipped; that had made her change her attitude and mind about the hood rat life. After that, she stayed where she belonged—out of the projects and with the other girls who would kiss her butt instead, on the other side of the street!

Karen's family was middle class. She was somewhat like me. We both could go to either the hood or the burbs and fit in well.

"So, what up, girl? I miss the rehearsal?" Anna asked.

"Yes you did." My lady rolled her eyes and laughed. "But, we can go over everything later."

Seeing Karen so happy felt good. Her happiness was all that I live for these days. I guessed my mother was right. I gave my all to my woman. They say that mother knows best.

"I thought your hubby was coming with you," Karen said.

"He did. I left him by the car when I saw you two. Here he comes now."

Her husband's name was Kevin Rinehart. He looked to be an average, well-paid white guy.

As we shook hands, I remembered that he'd once been in the military too.

"So, how's the ex-ranger doing?" he asked.

"Well I can't speak for you, but I need a drink," I stated as we both gave that powerful first handshake men do to see who is the strongest. "Well, let me say my good-byes to my family," I added. "My brother"—I pointed down the curb—"will take care of you, Kevin."

"Okay," he agreed. Then he turned to Anna. "I will call you later," he told her.

"If you do, then you must not be having a good time," Anna replied. "I do not want to talk to you until after you have a drink or two in you, okay?"

"You need to relax, Kevin."

"I will, he told his wife. Then he turned to me. "Hey, Jerry which one is your brother?"

"Yo, David," I called.

David looked up. I pointed to Kevin, and he understood. It had always been that way between me and my bother. We seemed to always know what the other was saying. But the same didn't apply to what the other was thinking! I was always two steps ahead of him. I made sure it was that way; I felt I had to be that way with all the people who surrounded me. I'd said it before and I'd say it many times more: Life is like chess, and I wasn't going to lose my place on the board to anyone. I knew that I might upset a few players, but that was the strategy that I used to get the upper hand.

The wind seemed to tell us all that we'd been outside a little too long. I saw a young, white couple huddled together walking in the direction of the church across the street. They were holding arms very close, and the young lady's hat came off. The wind blew it right into the street. Her knight in shining armor tried his best not to let it go too far in the lanes of traffic, but it was too late. A Chevy Tahoe ran over the. Being the gentlemen he was, the young man cleaned the hat off and placed it in his coat pocket. Then he took his hat off and placed it firmly atop his companion's head.

I tried to hurry my lady into the limousine, telling her to call me later. The snow was starting, and I urged her to please get out of the cold.

Karen was not having that at all. She wanted what all women want from their men—a lingering last—second look in his eyes and the words, "I love you."

As I spoke to Karen, I looked over to see my father and mother. I felt a sense of love between us all. "Mom, I will call you too in the morning, and I will be good."

"You had better," she said.

My mother knew me like a book, and I knew her. We'd spent a year living with each other during my final year of undergraduate studies, and she'd loved every minute of it. I had not lived with her since I was a boy of about nine or ten years old. So that year had given us the chance to get reacquainted with each other, and it seemed to me that we were never really apart.

Mom left me with a parting rendition of "Ain't Gonna Bump No More." "Don't bump with a big fat woman," she sang, laughing as she stepped into the car. Mom always had a song for the situation.

As for my father, David was actually my stepfather. He'd taken me in at the age of zero, and I called him Daddy. I had never really known my father, unless you counted the brief encounter we had in Savannah, Georgia, when all we'd done was argue. I didn't.

I assumed that my stepfather was coming with the boys and me. He was so proud of me. I had just graduated with an MBA, and a week later, I was getting married. My stepfather was as cool as the other side of the pillow. I could talk to him about anything. I didn't think there was a topic he was not well versed in. He knew it all but did not place himself above anyone.

Before I'd left to go into the army, he had told me, "Jerry, you control your life. No one else does." I had always remembered that piece of advice. And the most important thing he'd taught me was to never be a follower. I loved him very much. Even having gotten me out of the jams he'd had to help me with, he loved me like a son.

"Daddy, you coming?" I called.

"Hell yeah," he responded.

I smiled. Then I walked over to Karen to have my last kiss as an engaged man.

As we embraced, Karen whispered, "Please be good."

"I will," I said. "I promise." The look in my eyes told her I was not lying at all. "I will never leave you or hurt you. I told you that before." I then moved backward to let her retreat to her friends and family.

Karen turned and started moving toward Anna and her other friends. People were still coming out of the church, but I didn't really notice. I focused only on Karen as we said good-bye to the families. As I turned, I could see her mother waving that finger—he same one she'd waved at me when I'd asked Karen to marry me at the family picnic, on July 4 of this year.

That Fourth of July had been a blistering one. But even though the air was hot, the shade had made the afternoon feel relatively cool.

Teddy P. played in the background. My friends and some coworker's were there, but the majority of those gathered were Karen's family and friends. People danced; kids played Game Boys; and the air was filled with the sounds of a crowd running around, playing cards or dominoes or chess, and just plain, old trash-talking. Smoke rose from the grills in all directions, and other families like ours were out and about enjoying the day. I watched bikers making their way around the park and tourists walking through the grass and the flower beds filled with roses, tulips, and other beautiful flowers. It was one of those times when you knew that God was smiling at you and at this beautiful world that he created. I had just stepped away from the grill, where I'd talked with Karen's father and mother.

I had asked them would if it be okay that I stay in the family. They laughed, and Mr. Watson said impatiently, "Go get my daughter's hand in marriage." As I walked away, I looked over my shoulder just in time to see him wipe the tears from her mother's eyes as she smiled and waved that finger at me.

Karen had just returned from the Honey Child Salon and Spa. The salon was off LaSalle Street downtown, and we were at Grant Park not that far away.

As I knelt down on one knee, I asked her to have my mother's first grandchild from me and to be my wife.

I heard her friends scream in shock, and Karen screamed too, saying, "Yes."

As she jumped up and down, all of the females congregated around her. The men gathered around me, shaking my hand. She showed the ring, and I showed a smile.

✳　　✳　　✳

"Yo, Jay," David yelled out as I approached the driver's side of the Land Rover. "I know you're not going to drive tonight."

Everyone knew that I didn't like very many people driving me around. I only trusted a few people behind the wheel.

"So who's driving tonight?" David pressed. "It better not be Jerry."

I looked into the car and saw that Lay had already taken the seat and was not moving at all. Lay was one of the few who could take over my car and drive me somewhere—outside of my brother and Karen.

Chapter Two

Jerry's Night out with the Guys

"This night you gonna get drunk, sucked, and maybe you know what—if I can help it," Lay said.

"Yeah," Kelano and David cried out in agreement.

"You got everybody?" I asked David.

"I think so," he replied.

"Okay then. Come on, man. Let's get outta here and go to the *paaaaarty!*"

The friends and family were still getting into their vehicles across the street while looking at us pull off.

All the guys yelled out the windows, "Let's go!"

Off we went—four SUVs carrying six or seven grown men each. I was leaving a church and going to see naked women who were not my bride to be. I could only shake my head and laugh a little.

As I looked around the car, I noticed that only Kelano, David, Al, and Lay were with me in this car. Where was Anna's man, Kevin? I would get yelled at from here to the Hawaiian Islands.

"Where's my cell?" I asked David and Kelano.

"I got it," Kelano, blowing Dutch Master and weed into my face.

"All right now, dude, you know I don't smoke," I replied, sounding like a white boy.

We all laughed and gave each other dap. But it was true; I had quit smoking weed almost three years ago. I reached toward the back and received my cell phone from Kelano.

He started singing, "In hale, exhale; check out my flow."

Everybody laughed. They all loved me and wanted me to be relaxed and happy. I loved them too.

"Where is Anna husband?" I asked.

"Kelano, I told you to get him," David said.

"I did," Kelano replied, "and I put him in the car with your father."

Everybody clapped.

"Good one, dog," David said.

We started pouring drinks and talking about the old days. *I am glad they all came*, I thought to myself. It had been a long while since I'd seen them and since I'd felt this good. I *thank you, God, for this day and the many to come with Karen*. There had always been a void in my life, and I now know what was missing. If it wasn't for God bringing Karen to me, I knew I might still be going from country to country and living like a true nomad warrior.

"Turn the music down," I said. "I need to make this call."

"Why? Who you calling?" David and Lay asked together. "You're wifey?"

"Man, I'm trying to make sure we didn't leave wifey's girlfriend's husband," I replied.

"Naw," Kelano stated in his Turks and Caicos accent. "I grabbed that nerdy ass white boy up and put him in the last car."

"I know, but I want to make sure he is there, okay!"

"Yeah," Lay said, "I will keep him busy all night long and keep him outta your way. If that boy looks at you funny—like he's gonna tell on you, I will be taking him home ASAP!"

All I could do was smile. Lay had always been a kind of muscle for me. He was always ready to mess someone up. He'd made sure everything had gone well in Jacksonville. The Mexicans had loved him, and so did Sonya E., his woman. He made sure that he would be here regardless—even with the new fame Sonya had just acquired, mainly through the production and lyrics of "Myself."

Then there was Kelano. He was my right-hand man. We had hit it off from day one. We'd met in a weed spot. Both of us had been buying weed from this guy named Tony in Orlando. The next thing we knew, we were smoking together every day since—at least until I moved away to Jacksonville. Kelano and I had also gone to college together. We were friends for life. There was nothing I wouldn't do for my partner, Kelano.

Al was there too. Pretty Red was what we called him. He always makes jokes that red niggers were coming back in style. Man, he knew how to pull the ladies and how to make us laugh. He was my Artist Development man in Orlando and in Jacksonville.

I had my dogs and my brother with me. What more could I ask for?

As we approached Scores strip club, David placed his hand on my left shoulder and asked if I was ready for this.

"I been ready; are you?" I yelled, now feeling the weed and the cognac kick in.

They all started yelling and laughing, growing louder and louder. "Damn, how many people I got with me?" I joked. It felt like a gang in one car.

We all got out of the cars.

"About twenty to thirty," Lay said as he circled the front of the car, handing the keys to the valet. "I hope these boys act right. I mean if they don't, can I kick their asses?" he added with a smile.

Lay already knew what I was going to say. "Do what I would do."

With that, we all gathered outside the door.

"It is what it is when you live how I live." I gave them my entire boyish smile.

We heard the music as the door opened. I could not believe the club was playing one of my old jams. It sent me back to high school. "Yo, dog, you hear that?" I said to David.

The door closed behind the patrons who were entering the club, and the music disappeared.

"Yeah, this is going to be a good night," David replied. As always, my brother was reserved. Not much makes him get loud, unless he'd had too much to smoke and drink. Tonight was going to be that night. I knew that he would have too much to smoke and drink.

The door opened, and the song poured out again. "Here we go, Here we go, here we go, here we go, here we here we here we go D.M.C. and DJ Run"

"Dum diddy-dum diddy-diddy-dum dum," the guys chimed in in chorus.

"Now that is a classic," David said. "Run-D.M.C."

I remembered when Run-D.M.C. had first made an appearance on the music scene. "I was," I replied, "damn, I don't know how old, but I know I was young and dumb and full of . . . Well, we all know the rest of it, right . . ." My voice trailed off.

"Yeah, you need to let some of that go tonight," Kelano said with a laugh. Lay joined.

"Yo, Asaic, you all right?" Lay asked. David was also called Asaic.

"I'm good, dog."

"

"You need to get in there," Al said as we walked toward the door. "You know the guys brought you to a juicy ass, big titties club, right?"

"Hell yeah, I made sure to find the best strip club for you, Al," David said.

"Hey, Pops!" I called as Dad walked up with Mr. Watson.

"We're going to take a cab ride downtown—do it old man style and let you young boys here have a good time," Dad said. Then he turned to me. "Jerry listen, listen." My dad always repeated himself when he really wanted me to pay attention to what he said. "Watch out for each other, okay. Look out for David." He turned to David. "You look out for your brother. Okay, man, we out."

Mr. Watson gave me a hug and shook my hand. "Do not make me come look for your big self tomorrow, okay," he said.

"Don't worry. I will make sure he gets there," Al said to the both of them. Then he looked at me and said, "If you want to, we can leave now and go to Kelano's home island." We both laughed and started to walk toward the doors again.

I could see that Kevin was feeling a little out of place. So I spoke to him. "Hey, Kevin, you good?"

"Yeah, man, just let me at them," he replied.

We all took another look, watching the older men leave

"You pay for nothing," Asaic told me. "Everything is taken care of."

David is a one-of-a-kind brother, I thought to myself. David has in the past and still had a great life. He worked on one thing, and that one thing was keeping David alive.

I recalled my first visit to Boston to my little brother. As we walk toward the door, I thought about that trip.

✻ ✻ ✻

Man, I am in Beantown—Boston, Mass, I thought. As I exited the plane, I saw Dee.

"Dee. Yo, Dee," I called out over the crowded airport. "My man, my man."

"What's good?" Dika asked me.

"I'm good," I replied with a grin, "good at all the things I do and good at the things I'm to blame for too."

We hugged, and I noticed my brother wasn't coming up next to greet me. "Man, tell me, where the hell is Asiatic at?"

"I was on the other side of town by the airport, so I came by myself. I didn't tell him I was coming," Dika replied.

Then we heard, "Yo Jerry!"

I turned and saw David. "Man, I thought you weren't going to be here to greet your brother," I had to tease, with a big smile on my face.

I had not seen David for about seven years. I gave my little brother a hug, like I was hugging him for the last time in his life. I'd always worried about David. There was nothing that either one of us could tell each other that would make me not love and care for him. I will still be there for him.

"So what's the lineup?" I asked about my time with them both.

David eyed me, as if to let his gesture tell it all.

"All right, all right," I said. "I see I am in for a long weekend." I was giving both David and Dika dap. "Man, it is cold as hell in Florida," I joked. "I hope I can take the heat here in Boston." The temperature in Florida had been in the seventies when I'd left, and here in Boston it was in the lower teens.

"You going to freeze your ass off up here," Dika laughed.

"Yeah, bro, you brought some thermos I hope?"

"Naw, I don't need those in Jay-ville or Orlando. Just take me to the nearest Wal-Mart."

As we reached the car, I looked over to David. He nodded in a way that told me he felt the joy I was feeling and he agreed.

"I'll get with you boys later," Dika cried out as he jogged off toward his car.

"Yo, Dika," I called, "make sure you get with me at David's crib tonight."

"I will, I'll probably be there before you," Dika replied, now at the door of his Cadillac Escalade.

It was cold and snow was falling from a dark gray sky. It seemed to be just like Germany—cold, dark, and wet. I loved the cold, but this stuff was a still cold—no wind, no motion in the air at all. It was just plain old cold.

"My little bro must be coming up in the world," I said. "I mean driving a new 740 and all. This is nice." I touched the leather and adjusted the seat warmer.

"Yeah, but you pushing that big L. R.," David replied, referring to my Land Rover.

"Man, you know, you know," I said giving a fist and pointing up toward God.

The wood grain seemed to go all the way around the interior of the BMW, which was pearl white in color, with a dark tint and peanut butter guts to finish off the navigational system on deck. It was simple, and I could see he kept this car clean. My boy had made it in the game. He had put in work! "David, this is real nice, real nice," I said.

"I should start calling your ass Jerry two times," David said. "You keep repeating yourself."

"I just watched the mobster movie *Good Fellows*."

We laughed.

"You know how they do it. Man, I need a hook."

"What's a hook?" David asked.

"It's a shot. I need a shot. Take me by a liquor store. I need some Hennessy—one that I can do right now!"

David turned right at the corner, and there my request was—Latino Liquors. The area was filled with old, dilapidated buildings. This was the east side of town, and it reminded me of New York. The smell of urine and trash was in the air. On the same corner was the typical hangout crew in front of the liquor store. Snow was everywhere, and the mixture of asphalt, dirt, and oil mixed in made the area more urban and at home for me. I never lived in a bad area, but it seemed I'd spent so much of my time in the projects or in hard times areas that that's where I felt at home.

"You good, boy; you on point!" I smiled and moved to get out of the car.

David got out, and this was the first time I noticed how clean he was. He wore fresh, new timberlands, Rocawear jeans, an FUBU shirt, and a phat ass Phat Farm leather jacket—all in black—and he wore a platinum Jesus cross on his chest.

"Yeah," I added, "that was a tight move. I really need to get a drink and see the hood. I feel at home."

"Right, I knew you would," David replied. "You up here on some gangster stuff anyway. You should feel at home. Where the hell is the stuff you brought for me?"

I just gave him a look.

"For real, what you got for me?" David pressed.

I didn't say anything.

"Man, come on. Let's get something to drink."

"You need any loot?" I asked.

"Naw," he replied. "I'm good."

"You always say that."

"Say what?" he asked.

"I'm good. That is like your signature answer to me when I ask if you need anything," I answered as we walked in the store.

"Well, I am," he said. "If I need something from you, I will ask."

"Yeah you right," I joked. "When am I going to get my five grand back anyway?" I knew I would never see that five again.

"I got you, bro," David laughed. He smiled gave me a pound.

"Yeah, as long as you got me I'll never be broke, right," I snarled in a joking manner. "What you drinking on?"

"You know me. It's got to be Hennessey!" David said. "Hold on, bro. My phone is ringing." He flipped his phone open. "Yo, this Dee. Yeah . . ." David walked away as I went toward the counter.

"Hey, where are your half gallons of the good stuff?" I asked the attendant, not interested in the variety lined up behind the counter. "I needed to get a choicer brand of cognac—something more upscale."

I turned to see that David was still on the phone. He was walking through the aisles of the store.

"You still with that Spanish girl?" I asked him.

He nodded his head yeah.

I saw a girl walking down the same aisle as my brother. She was a fine piece of a lady.

"She live with you?" I asked.

"Naw, dog, you know better than that." He folded his cell phone. "I got to be by myself just like you."

"Yeah," I said. But the truth was that I hated being without a steady woman. It seemed that I was sleeping around too much and that I was cheating myself out of having a full life. I mean God made woman from man's rib. A man without a woman in his life was not complete.

I turned back to the attendant and repeated my question. "Where is the good cognac?

He pointed toward the end of the last aisle.

"Dee." I pointed over to the last row.

"Now what is this?" I had to say in a low tone. The girl I'd noticed earlier was coming back up the aisle. She was a beautiful Spanish woman. I asked her name.

She smiled. "My name is Isabella." She was all of five foot eight and about 160 pounds. She was very sexy and very not looking at me with eyes of intention. She was thick, and there wasn't an inch of body fat on her.

"Excuse me, let me introduce myself," I said to her.

She spoke in Spanish, as if to tell me that she was not interested. She shocked when I spoke Spanish back to her. Her mood changed. "I don't speak very good English," she said, smiling from ear to ear.

"I don't either," I said to lighten the conversation.

As we talked, I could feel someone come up behind me. "Jay, you ready. We got to go."

"Okay." I gave David the bottle and my money to take care of the drinks he and I wanted and reached in my pocket for one of my business cards for Isabella. "I design a line of clothing for women and men called 'All Me'."

"Oh yeah," she replied. "I have some of your workout outfits."

"You do, do you?" She made me smile. I knew that David was putting my line out here in Boston. "Isabella, here is my number," I said in Spanish. "I am here for a week and would like to spend some of this time with you."

She smiled and agreed. "I'll call you tonight about ten. Maybe we can meet up." Isabella's tone and her Spanish were sexy.

"That is something that I will be looking forward to," I replied. "But first, why are you here? What do you drink?"

"That we can talk about tonight when I call," she replied. She took out her phone and looked at my card. "Is this your cell?" she asked. When I replied in the affirmative she told me she'd call me now.

She finished dialing, and my phone rang. "If I don't call on time, you call me," she said.

"Okay," I agreed. "That is a plan."

We shook hands, and I walked out of the store. As we got to the car, David looked over the top of the car. "I can't take your pimping ass anywhere," he said shaking his head. "I saw her and knew you were going to ask her for her number."

"I didn't ask for her number," I replied. "I just put my gift of gab on in Spanish, and all she could do was 'Cream / Get on Top.'" I sang the Prince lyrics.

David laughed.

As we pulled off, I could see Isabella looking out of the front door and waving bye.

"Yeah, boooyyyy!" I knew I had her.

"Anyway, what time is it?" David asked me.

"One forty-five. Why? Oh, your stuff. Is that what you are talking about?"

"Yeah, dog. What's good?"

"Go to 1208 Boston Boulevard," I told him.

"Why? Who lives there?" David asked.

"Man, just take your ass over there."

As David pulled up to the block I'd instructed him to go to, he asked. "Why are we here? And how are you and Marissa?"

"There ain't no me and Marissa." I told him. "I let that go months ago. I can't keep being with a girl who doesn't love herself. Peace of mind is peace of mind, and I need a piece of mine. I mean she was a good girl and all, but I need more. I don't like girls with a lot of issues. It seems all Florida girls want money or you to take care of their assets."

"Man, that's everywhere," David said.

I paused for a second. "Yeah, it does seem to be like that everywhere." I grabbed for the door handle, opened the door, and walked off.

As we approached Scores. The strip club.—David placed his hand on my left shoulder and asked was I ready for this. I've been ready, are you—I yelled, now feeling the cognac kick in. Damn how many people I got with me.

I asked Lay as he got out the car and as I stepped down on the concrete outside of the strip club.

About 30 to 40 Lay said as he circled the front of the car handing the keys to the valet. I hope these boys act right. Lay said. I mean if they don't can I kick their asses? Lay smiled as he asked me that question.

Lay already knew what I was going to say.

It is what it is, when you live how I live. I gave them all my entire boyish smile . . . .

I heard the music as the door open from the club. I could not believe they were playing one of the old jams. It sent me back to high school. Yo dog you hear that? I said to David. Yeah this is going to be a good night. As always David is well reserved. Not too much makes him get loud, unless he had to much to smoke and drink.

The door open and the song began again. Here we go, Here we go, here we go, here we go, herieeee go . . . . it's DMC and DJ Run—dumb, ditty, dumb, ditty, ditty, dumb dumb . . . . we all yelled out—Now that is a classic David said. Run DMC.

I remember when they first came out. I replied. I was—damn I don't know how old but I know I was young and full of dum stuff in my mind. Yeah you need to let some of that go tonight.

Kelano laughed along with lay. I need to get in here; Al called out from tha back of the group. I know you guys brought me too a juicy sexy ass club. Right? Al said as I walked towards my brother. Hell yeah . . . . I made sure to find the best strip club for you. David said laughing like it was all for AL. As we all walked into the door I looked back. I felt something on the back of my neck. It seems that I was being watched. I always seem to think that way sense Puerto Rico at the Ritz Carlton San Juan Casino and Spa. That is a time that made my life change. I am so glad Karen stayed with me after the two weeks. Well that is a story for another time.

Chapter Three

Karen's Night with the Ladies!

Jerry and the men were gone, and I was looking forward to the evening with my girls. Shivering in the freezing air, I hurried to the limousine. Just as I put my hand on the cold door handle, someone called my name.

I walked away from the door to see what my friend, Kim, needed.

"Hey, girl! Am I riding with you?" Kim asked.

"You better believe it, baby." I turned and headed back toward Anna and the limousine. Sam was waiting at the door with Anna. People were still coming out of the church, but I didn't notice them.

"So, Sam, what brings you here with us tonight?" I looked at Sam, expecting a lie.

"I came here to see if this was real," Sam replied in her street voice. "Girl, you are so lucky to have a man like Jerry." Sam was smart, but the hood ran her and how she acted everywhere. She was what we all knew as a hood rat with a good federal job.

"You and I both know that," I replied.

Kim-2 turned up the music in the limo and leaned her head out of the car door, where Sam and I were talking. "Karen, get in this car," she said. "It's too cold to be out there talking just to be talking."

Rachel held out the bottle of bubbly. "Look, you have to be in here to get this," she said. She took a glass and gave the bottle to Anna.

Anna got into the limo.

"And he is all my man!" I said, holding Sam's gaze. "I just wanted you to remember that and know that, okay?"

"Yeah, girl, you know that I am not tripping on your man. Jerry and I are just coworkers."

I could feel the tension in Sam's statement, but, I took it in stride. While my girls in the car waited, I glared at Sam. "Yeah you are so right about that," I said. "But I can understand if you're unhappy," I added. "Any dumb woman who let a man like Jerry slip through her fingers deserves to be upset—a whole hell of a lot." I eyed the girls in the car, knowing I'd gotten the best of Sam. "I mean he is handsome, tall, smart, and successful. He has a damn good job, making all kinds of good money, and he has a big, thick joystick."

As I spoke, I felt like it wasn't just Sam but my entire group who wanted some of Jerry. I could be wrong. I knew I was just upset at seeing this trifling woman.

"Karen, you need to stop," Anna broke in. "Jerry isn't all that."

"If you knew you too would want a piece," I snapped, loud and proud, looking dead at Alicia, who readjusted herself in her seat next to Kim-2, uncrossing her legs and closing them quickly.

"Well all I know is you caught him at the right time," Kim-2 stated.

"I sure did," I replied sharply.

"How long was he here again—I mean living here in Chicago?" Sam asked, as if she didn't know. "Was it about three to five months?"

I didn't remember how long Jerry had been in Chicago when we met, but I knew why Sam was asking the question. *This little something something wants to start something, and I damn well am ready to finish it*, I thought.

"Get your behind in the car," my mom, who'd came out of nowhere, told me, closing the almost fight down. "You girls are going to get sick, and nobody's going to make it to the wedding tomorrow. We can do all our talking when we get in the rooms."

Sam turned to get into the limousine and was met with an arm. "I think your ride is the last car!" Rachel knew the whole story and wanted to keep things cool. "Anna, do you still wanting to be the maid of honor?" she asked once Sam was gone.

"Move over, girl. Let Karen in," Renee added, changing the subject

Anna, being very wise to the atmosphere, said, "I meant to ask you about that. I don't mind sharing the job if that's okay with Karen."

They both looked over at me.

"I have no problem with that at all," I replied, snarling out my words.

"Look at you, pulling your hair over to the side like you're about to do something. We all know your ass cannot fight," Alicia stated, clearly hoping to lighten the mood.

I laughed. "Yeah, but she doesn't!"

"Let me move over here by the door to get a better look at Sam," Rachel said, still trying to break the thick fog that was lifting in the air.

"Yeah, I didn't want to have to put the grease on and take off these fake nails tonight." Said Rachel

"What do you mean?" Rachel looked away then

"OMG!" Anna said. "You just might have to anyway. Here this woman comes again. Karen, let me handle this."

Anna got out the car and said a few words to Sam. Then Sam walked away.

I wanted to be the next center of attention here. Kimsaid while getting into the car

Rachel touched my arm, getting my attention so I wouldn't be looking out at Sam. I could see Anna sticking out her tongue and grinning to lighten the mood while Sam walked away.

Anna got into the vehicle, and the ladies looked at her. Then the limo filled with laughter, and the tension was gone—well enough to go on with another conversation. As Anna and Rachel discussed what they would do about getting Anna something in a matching color and style as the other girls in the ceremony, Kim-1 and the others talked to me to keep my mind right. This was a time for me, and I'd be damned if anyone was going to make it a bad night. I started to just lay back and think about Jerry. But there was too much catching up and fun with my girls to talk about tonight.

My entourage and I had left in the Navigator limos, pearl white. As we pulled away, the music of Stevie Wonder filled the air. The music was so loud I could barely hear myself think. In the limo with me were Alicia and Renee, my two sisters, along with Anna, my old school buddy, who was as loud and wild as always. I'd put money on Anna making this night really different than the others would. Also there was my sister from another mother, Kim Merritt (aka Kim-2 or K-2). K-2, my fraternity sister, was blessed heavily in the breast area, but she had a small fame. She stood about six feet three inches and talked as if she was always lost. But one shouldn't be fooled. She was a self-made, seven-figure woman and very down to earth. Kim Willis had been my girlfriend since grade school. People got the Kims mixed up when we talked about them, so we called her Kim-1. Tonya was a college friend of Kim-2's and mine, and she was reliable. She was the type or person you could call for anything because she knew how to get it and she had the connections in the hood. She made it happen, dang it! That was my homey! What I liked the most about Tonya was that she was cool as heck.

Then there was Rachel. Now this was the one girl I knew would be by my side day in and day out. She had been since college, and we would always be best friends. She did not get into everybody's business, and she was the only girl here who handled her men like you saw divas do in movies. She didn't give them much, but they spoiled her plenty.

Another Navigator limo followed with my mother, my aunts, and some cousins, along with Jerry's mother, his sisters, and one aunt. In the car limo were Sam, Jackie, Angela, Ashley, and two other women who were friends of the families.

As we rode down Financial Street, Anna asked, "So where are we going? And what time is the wedding?"

Kim-2 turned down the music.

"Jerry and I wanted a late evening wedding, with candles and fire sticks," I answered. "Anyway, I know my man, and he might not even drink tonight so that he can be on point, or as he says it, two steps ahead of everybody.

"So, Anna," I asked, changing the subject as I sat up straight to receive my glass of champagne, "how does it feel to be back in America. I mean you have not been here in how long?"

"It's been about six years." Anna sipped on her drink and bounced to the tunes in the background, waving her hand over her head. "I don't mind not coming home that often because I love making that money."

"I see you have not slowed down your drinking either."

"Money and drinking are like kids and a headache, girl. They go together."

I looked around to make sure that Sam wasn't in the car. I knew she wasn't, but I guess I was just tripping. I didn't mind if Sam came with us girls because I wanted to keep both of my eyes on her. She was fast and hot for my man's body. It wasn't that I feared Sam; I didn't at all. But I had to wonder what this stink behind woman wanted. She'd been at my wedding rehearsal, and now she was in the car following us to the bachelorette party. I couldn't wait to see how this night was going to end. I'd noticed that Sam had been looking at Jerry during the entire rehearsal, and I knew she was up to something. I couldn't wait to tell Anna!

Wait a minute, I stopped myself. *I can't tell Anna that Jerry slept with Sam. It would get too ugly too fast around here.*

I'd have to tell Rachel and Kim-2, though. They were my best friends. But they might not like the fact that I was letting Sam around us. I decided I was going to have a little fun with my girls and my family. I would let them in on what was really good later. I was going to forget about Sam and wait until it was the right time to let her have it.

I was happy to see that Rachel and everyone else had made it. Rachel had thought she wasn't going to be here on time. As the sales director for Coca-Cola in Atlanta, Georgia, she worked very hard, and at first, she hadn't been sure if she'd be able to take time off at all. But she had made it, and I had two maids of honor—Rachel and Anna. Ever since she'd arrived, Rachel had worked to make sure everything was in place. I watched her now chatting it up, and I was so happy she was here.

I wondered whether Jerry's friend from Atlanta had made it here yet. He hadn't said anything to me. But that was Jerry's way. He tried not to let me know that he cared about his friends as much as he really did. I decided I'd call him later and ask him about his friend then.

Then out of the blue Anna asked me, "So, Karen, tell me again, what happened to Leroy?"

"Anna, please don't start that conversation up again," Kim-2 said.

"Who's Leroy?" Tonya asked.

"That man is a hunk—sexy, older, and he has his own practice," Anna stated loudly so that all could hear.

Kim-2 tried to turn the music back up, but Anna jumped over and grabbed Kim-2's hand laughing. Someone turned the music off in the back.

"Look, Anna," I said, "you've been drinking too fast. You'll be asleep in about another hour if you don't slow down or quit."

"You want to bet? I can hold mine. Now tell everybody how you use to hold Leroy's ears." She burst into laughter.

Everyone in the car laughed, and I couldn't help but join in. "Now, ladies," I began, "what I say here stays in this car! I love Jerry, and money is not everything." If these ladies really knew about my man, they would leave this issue where it needed to be—DEAD! But I knew that wasn't going to happen. And I felt like telling the story again. *Girl, girl, girl*, I thought to myself, *what a time I had with Leroy.*

"Yes it is, girl!" Anna said, with a roar of laughter and a huge smile. "Money is the root to your sexual satisfaction!"

The girls all laughed and gave each other high fives, and we shared another round of champagne.

"Look," I told my friends, smiling for their company and the champagne and the memories, "Leroy was a good time for awhile, but it would not and could not work for me and him. I'm telling you, Dr. Feelgood is in the past. I do not miss him at all."

"What?" Anna protested. "You are such a liar. Girls, she used to call me in Japan and brag about how good the D-I-C-K was." She made a gesture indicating the size of Leroy's dick and licked her lips to emphasize how much she liked my stories.

"I knew I should have not told this one here," I giggled. "But she was all the way overseas. I never knew it would come back in my face. Who was I lying to? Oh well."

"Tell the truth, girl. It will set you free and make us horny!" Rachel replied.

"Hell, yeah, it will," Anna said.

I hated doing this now because of the wedding, but we did need something to talk about until we got to the room. I could now feel the warmth of the vehicle, and the drinks that I'd had made me take off my coat. This caused a chain reaction with the other women. I could see what they all were thinking: *Okay, this must be a good story. She is taking off her coat.*

I shook my head at Anna. "I can't believe you brought this up now. I was just getting my buzz on."

"Well, hell, then you should feel like telling it," Kim-2 said.

"I do!" I smiled. "Now be quiet while I take all of you on a journey down my memory lane."

All ears were trained on me, and someone turned the music off completely now.

"As we all know, women cannot let a juicy story go by," I said, taking a sip of champagne and looking around at all of them. "So, my merry lot, here it goes.

"I was in my last days at Howard. The weather was perfect, and I felt like I was on the top of the world."

"She will be in a few," Kim-2 cut in with a laugh.

"That afternoon was my graduation, and I was walking over to the café to get some bottled water for my family before they arrived.

"Girl, just tell us the dang ole story!" Rachel said.

"Okay, Okay," I replied. "Leroy was there with his son and ex-wife. That was the first time I saw him. Leroy stood all of six four and had the body of Morris Chestnut."

"Yeah and you wanted his chestnuts," Tonya said.

The ladies laughed.

That was not funny, I thought to myself. So I just rolled my eyes, smiled at Tonya, and continued.

"He had a goatee with those salt and pepper hairs all over. Anyway, as I left the dorm, I spotted him, and he winked at me. I didn't think anything of it at all. After the ceremony, my family and I went to dinner. Then I left them in their room so that they could get some rest and I could go out with my friends. Alicia, Renee, Tonya, and Kim-2, I don't even remember where you were Ann. I said as I got on the elevator . . ."

"Yes!" Kim-2 screamed out, a look of recognition gleaming in her eye. "That was Leroy?"

I giggled a little and replied, "Yep. Once we were in the elevator, we did the small chitchat thing. When the door opened on the ground level, I didn't even notice I'd missed my floor. I was going to change into some jeans.

I really wanted to stop there because I felt that I may have said too much already, but I also wanted to tell this story. So I continued. "Well ladies . . ."

"Come on, baby, spill the beans. How did he look again?" Kim-1 asked.

I blushed and told them about how I could tell he had charm just by looking at him, how charisma just leaped from his eyes and words. As I spoke, I could see Leroy again in the elevator and smell his cologne. "He was dressed in this Armani suit, and his shoes were hot," I told them. "I love a man with big feet, and his shoes were clean and ready," I screamed out loud, losing myself in the memory.

Rachel looked at me. "Hot?!" she said. "What was hot about his shoes?"

"I don't know. I just have a thing for men in nice-looking shoes," I replied. "Now let me finish, girl."

"Yeah let her tell it like it is. Was it his shoes or his shoe size you were looking at?" Anna said lustily.

"Girl, shut up and let me finish what I didn't want to start."

"Well get to the good part," Renee requested.

"As we left the elevator, he asked if I would like to have a drink with him. I didn't hesitate but came back with a yes before he could say another word. I must admit I said it kind of quickly."

I eyed everyone in the limo. I knew that they all were ready to hear the story now. Looking at my watch, I saw that I did have a little time to spare. *Why not?* I thought.

"As we sat and talked, he insisted that I look as good as Halle Berry. Well I knew that was a pickup line, and I just played it off. When the drink was over, he asked me to have another, and I agreed. The lounge in the Crown Plaza had an earthy feel.

"Naw! It was that scooter between your legs that had that earthy feel about it," Anna roared.

The car filled with hoots and hollers as the girls burst into laughter, tears streaming down some of our faces. I could barley stop laughing.

"Anyway, he had told me about his son, Garrett, and said that we were the same age. That didn't make me feel any better about talking to this man twice my age. But he was so charming."

"And don't forget charismatic," Kim-2 said with a big Ronald McDonald smile.

"Before I knew it, we'd been talking for awhile, and I'd had one too many merlots. I could feel the drink, so I stood up ready to go. He held my arm to keep me balanced. It was strong. His arm reminded me of my father's when he was helping me learn how to ride my bike, but he was as gentle as a kiss on the cheek from your grandmother."

"Oooohh," the girls all replied in sync.

"As we walked, I laid my head on his arm because his shoulder was over my head. I felt a little dizzy from my drinks. He kept saying, 'I got you. I would not let you fall.' I knew

he wouldn't, and if he did, I was going to have a lot to say."
I giggled and gave Anna a high five. "Somebody pour me a drink, please. All this talking is making me thirsty."

I accepted a refill in my glass and then continued. "At my door, I placed the card in, and before I knew it, he was walking in behind me. I made my way to the bed, and he sat at the desk near the phone. He took off his jacket and hung it in the closet. I asked him what he was doing. 'I just wanted to make sure my jacket doesn't wrinkle,' he said. 'Is that ok?' I couldn't fight with him. He had me dizzy and gazing into his eyes. I was like a lost puppy in need of guidance. We talked a little more, and I again began to feel warm inside for this man. I kept thinking that he was forty-something years old, but the more we talked, the more I wanted him inside me. He called up for a bottle of merlot, and I didn't stop him. I was lying on the bed, but I got up and walked over to him at the desk. I placed my hand on his shoulder and let him know that I had to change and also that I was going to take a shower."

"Yeah, you wanted that snatch fresh, huh?" Anna laughed, her eyes waiting for a response.

But she didn't receive one from me. I just kept telling the story. "As I bathed, I sang the Luther Vandross song, "If Only for One Night." And then I heard the door. Room service had brought up the wine, sushi, and oysters. I could see the room from the shower mirror. It seemed that I turned my head for just a minute, and he was at the shower door undressed, his manhood standing at attention and ready to greet me. I didn't even hear him come into the bathroom. And I didn't stop him from coming into the shower.

"He stepped into the shower, all six foot four and, by my guess 240 pounds of him. We reached out and met each other with a passionate kiss. He delivered another to my shoulder then to my breast. Then he knelt down and placed one of my legs on his shoulder. I can remember moaning wildly while he lifted me up, holding me in the center of the shower."

Renee, Anna, and Kim-1 moaned while I told the story.

"I remember that he placed a finger in my hot, wet spot. I could no longer see his face. He then licked me all over my juicy walls of pleasure. I held on to the shower rod with both hands. He took me by surprise when he placed my second leg on his other shoulder. The water hit me on my back, and it made my hot spot even wetter. Leroy grabbed both my ass cheeks and pulled me closer. I felt his tongue go deeper in me, and I placed one of my hands on the back of his head. I thought that I was going to hit the ceiling. I grabbed for both sides of the shower to keep us balanced. His tongue kept a steady pace that made me feel like this was the first time someone had gotten it right! I refused to let him stop; I humped his face over and over."

I paused then looked over at Alicia and said loudly, "I came so hard I thought that I would knock us both out of the shower. But Leroy just held on and let me down a little so that I could take a ride on his pink, hot, short-range missile. And for any of you who got lost, I'm referring to the man's tongue. He then lifted me up and down over and over until I came again. Stay with me, girls!"

Every woman in the car was moist and bothered. They all wanted to be me, and they all wanted my Leroy.

"As he let me down, I was compelled to kiss my own love juices. He moved my hair to the side then turned me around in a slow motion while keeping me level. I bent over. Then, girls, I woke up. It was all a dream." I roared with laughter.

"Come on, tell the truth. This is all a dream? You made it up?" Kim-2 asked quickly. "What happened?" I could tell from Kim-2's eyes and body language that her body wanted to hear more and wanted to have sex. I was sure she felt as if Leroy was a man who she wouldn't have left. But I am glad that I have Jerry. He is all the man I need. I stated to myself.

"No, it was not a dream. I will tell you all the rest, but you better not ever tell Jerry."

"Go ahead and tell the story," Anna said. "I know what happened. He gave you that entire manhood, huh?"

"Yes, he did," I said to them, all smiles, while waving my hand in front of their faces as if they were hot and I was fanning them.

"He and I both grabbed the showerhead as he pushed in and out slowly, getting all of him in me. He took his time and made sure to not hurt me." I thought about how good it had felt and began to get wet in the limo, thinking nothing of Jerry at that time. "Girls, I tell you, when all that was all up in me, I screamed! I'd never had a man so big and so tender all at the same time. He knew what I wanted. It started out slow like I like it, and then he kept it at the same pace. I came again and again. I don't know how many times, but if you count those half ones, it was a lot." I burst into laughter again.

"Did you please him?" Tonya asked.

"Yes I did, but I kept coming, and he didn't."

"No, girl, did you give him a treat?"

"Yes. Wait and I'll tell you. You see, he didn't have an organism at that time."

"What? He didn't?" someone yelled.

"No, that man has control!" I told them. "As we had intense, doggy-style sex standing, I felt him pull back and turn me again. I felt his piece by my leg, and I placed him in me again. It seemed as if he wanted to get out of the shower, but I didn't. I wrapped my legs around him and held on. He pushed, and with a thrust of pressure, I felt the pleasures of him again. He was strong, hard, and ready—black coffee, no sugar. Then he poured out a lot of cream in me.

"We washed each other. I put on my robe, and he put on a towel. We ate, drank, and talked—you know, small talk about where I was going after this. I informed him that I was moving back to Chicago. I had done an internship there and the company wanted me back to start next week. He said he'd be in Chicago that next month, and he would like to see me again. I agreed. He pulled at my leg, and I came over to him on the floor. I gave him oral because I felt that he deserved it, and he enjoyed my services.

"We wiped each other down again, and I noticed that the floor was soaking wet, from the curtain to the floor."

"How did you two get to the curtains?" Kim-1 asked.

"I have no idea! Well I sat on the chair to wipe the floor, but then I couldn't stop myself. I walked into the bathroom and sat on the toilet, watching him getting dressed. As I sat there on the toilet, I gave him head again—the best I could muster up."

"Karen, you are a freaky little thing, aren't you?" Alicia said, smiling.

"You know I don't do that really," I told everyone in the car, a smile on my face again. I waved my hand from left to right, stating that I was telling the truth. "Something just came over me," I said, trying not to giggle and trying to be sincere.

"But you did and you did it twice," Alicia said, rolling in her seat with laughter. "Oohh," she hooted. "I'm gonna tell Momma."

Renee laughed.

"I wanted to please him as he had me," I replied. "He did, so I did. Then he came once again on me. He said he could not do that to me—not in my mouth."

"He treated you like '*a lady*,'" Tonya said, doing her best Martin Lawrence.

All my girls laughed, and we shared another drink.

"You got those DSLs. That's why," Angela said.

The vehicle shook, and laughter rang out again. We were having such a good time I was sure that the people in the car next to us stopped at the traffic light could hear laughter poured out from the limo.

"Well you know what happened after that?" I asked.

"No we do not," said Kim-1.

"I want to know more," Rachel said. She too—like all my girls—was getting a little hot in the lower regions of her panties. As was I.

"Driver, where is the liquor?" Anna screamed out. "Turn the music back up a little."

The driver responded, telling us the liquor was in the bottom right cabinet.

"Girl, I think the driver was listening to your story the whole time," Anna said. "Driver, were you listening to my girlfriend's story?"

The driver got quiet for a second. Then he said, "Yes, I was I was going to tell you ladies we were here—I mean at the hotel—but the story was just getting good. I need me a man like that."

"What's your name?" Rachel asked him.

"My name is Harry."

"*Ooohh*, you said you need a man, right? Rachel asked again. And what?!" Harry replied. I need me a man like that Leroy or whateva his name is! Harry snapped his fingers swirled his head around to place his feet on the brake and then looked back at us, and said, "A man can't get good love from a man no more."

Everyone in the limo—from the front to the rear—was in tears laughing so hard.

"Is there more, Karen?" Harry asked over the screams and laughing.

"Turn your behind around and drive," Anna said.

"Girl, we are here at the hotel! I've been going around the block for twenty-five minutes!" Harry clapped his hands, snapped his fingers, and said, "Helllar heller," just like Madea! "So, if you ladies are ready to go, I will get the bags and the door."

We all started getting our things in order, and Harry walked around to open the door. My ladies all looked at each other, and

I made sure to catch each of their eyes before saying, "Okay, ladies, whatever we do here, it does not get back to your men or my Jerry, okay."

They all agreed, and I looked down to find the door handle.

Just I was about to grab the handle, Harry opened the door. "Welcome, ladies, to the Hard Rock Café, downtown Chicago."

"Girl, I thought we were going to the Waldorf?" Kim-1 said, her tone a question.

"No, I changed it at the last minute so that Karen couldn't tell Jerry," Rachel told her.

This made Kim-1 smile from ear to ear.

The front doors opened to the lobby area. My mom and Jerry's mom were seated, waiting for us to arrive. Sam and the other women were at the bar having a drink and keeping the bartender's attention.

I felt that I shouldn't have told the girls about Leroy. But it had all happened before Jerry, and he knew about Leroy anyway—well not everything.

"Hey, baby," my mom said greeting me, "you girls stop off somewhere?"

"No, mother, we just got caught in traffic. That's all," I told her.

I smiled at Jerry's mom. "Hi, Mrs. Jones. Have you been waiting too long?"

My future mother-in-law smiled back. "No, baby. I just need to go upstairs and get my things in my room. I think I'll turn in and see you girls later. Sonya and Sandra will be down to the party."

"Okay, Momma," Sonya said, coming up to the table, "I got our rooms, and Sandra got the bellboy to take the bags up. You ready?"

"Okay," Mrs. Jones replied. Then she turned back to me. "Let me say good night to your mother, Karen."

"Sonya, you and your sister are coming to the room, right?" Karen asked.

"Girl, please, you better believe it," Sonya replied. "I'm ready to have some fun. My flight from New York was too hard on me."

"I can't wait for you to get to know the girls," I beamed.

"Yes," Anna said with a grin. "We have a lot to ask you about Jerry."

As Mrs. Jones and her daughters walked into the elevator, Anna walked back over to me.

"Jerry's sisters are really polite, and they take good care of their mother, as does Jerry," I told her. "I like them both."

"Well, that's a good thing, girl. There is nothing worse then your sister-in-law not liking you and you not liking her back. Is Jerry's mother okay?"

"Yeah, she just needs some rest."

"Baby, I'm going up with Mrs. Jones. We have rooms close by each other. I'll be down in awhile with her. Or we might take a cab to the mall down the street."

"The one on Michigan?" I asked.

She replied in the affirmative and I told her I'd talk to her later.

"Bye, Mother Watson," Rachel, Anna, Tonya, and the Kims said in chorus.

Alicia and Renee left to help their mother to her room.

"Rachel, you got the keys?" Tonya asked, referring to the key to the suite we ladies would be sleeping in. "How many rooms in this place?"

"It has three bedrooms," Rachel replied. "And we have it until Monday."

Sam eyed Karen and her friends, anger rising in her body. *This cow thinks that is the end of this*, she told herself. *I know better. I'm gonna get her ass in the end. Jerry needs me. I have put up with women like this all my life. They come in and think their stuff doesn't stink.*

Sam knew Jerry didn't love Karen the way Karen told it. She thought about Savannah and how she and Jerry had shared a great weekend. She knew they'd decided not to tell anyone (though she had done so anyway). *But I love him and he loves me*, she thought. *And no little, cute ass, goody-two-shoes is going to have him.* She knew that Jerry loving her was enough. She would just sit back and bide her time and then leap on the situation at the right moment.

Maybe I'll go by his crib tonight in something nice and see-through, she contemplated. She thought about waiting in the dark in his room and seducing him. He would like that.

Sam looked over at Karen. The girls from Sam's table had joined the main group now. *She knows she wishes she could be me*, Sam told herself. *I really have his heart. If I just would have slowed down like he'd asked me, we would be together.*

"This is far from over. I promise you that," she said under her breath, her gaze trained on Karen. Then she walked over in front of the group.

✳   ✳   ✳

"What floor are we on?" I asked Rachel.

"The top, baby," she grinned. "We have two suites and each has three bedrooms." Then she turned to the crowd of girls. "Look, ladies, we are just going up here for a minute to relax. Then we are going to the club. So go wash, change, and meet back in the lobby at ten. If you are late, you will be catching a cab. The limos will be gone by ten-oh-five."

Rachel, being the organizer that she was, was getting everybody in line, and all I had to was enjoy myself and look good. I loved my girl.

Look at this, I thought to myself, as I noticed a girl with the red hair. *She must be with Sam.* I was ready to get in the shower, and I wondered what my baby was doing now. He was so sweet to me. I looked down at my ring—four karats. I had never thought that I would be with a man like this. Every woman dreamed of finding a man like Jerry, of having a day like today and like the one I was going to have tomorrow. But not many dreams came true. Tomorrow, my dream would. I would not let anything stop that from happening—nothing at all!

My girls were loud in the elevator. Damn, I wished Anna would chill out a little. But that was asking too much of her.

All I could do at this moment was think of Jerry—my man, my best friend, my husband, my love.

"Here's your key, Karen," Rachel said, handing me the card as we made our way to the door. "In the main room, I have me, Kim-2, and Karen. Kim-1, Anna, and Tonya, you three are in the other room."

"Where are your sisters staying, Karen?" Tonya asked.

"They have their own room together downstairs somewhere."

"Oh, okay that's cool with me," Anna replied.

Rachel opened our door, and we walked in. The two rooms were connected.

"Hey, you funny, girl. You got the rooms together for us all," Kim-1 said.

"Yeah, Kim," Rachel said. "How're we going to have fun in separate rooms?"

"Well where is the bar?" Kim-1 asked.

"Look it's over there." Anna said

"I want a drink." Kim-1 said

"I want to sit." Rachel said

"I want a shower." Alicia said

"Me too." Tonya said

"There are four bathrooms in here, so let's get the butt-washing in motion," Rachel directed.

"I'm ready for the club," Anna hooted.

"Anna, we know that you're ready for the club," Rachel replied. "But please wash your behind. You just got off the plane from Japan." She turned to me. "I need to call your sisters-in-law and tell them about the time we're leaving."

"No, I'll call them now," I told her.

"Okay, girl," she replied, smiling at me. "I guess I'll go unpack a few things. You need me to unpack your things for tonight?"

"No, Rachel. I don't know what I'm going to wear yet. Let me call Sandra and Sonya."

Chapter Four

RTE

We ladies began to laugh as we road down Interstate 294. We'd had a good time up in the room, and now it was time to have a good time at the club.

"Rachel, where you have us going?" Anna asked.

"We're going to RTE."

"I've heard of that place. Isn't that where all the sports stars go?"

"Yes!"

"Girl, for someone from Atlanta, you know a lot about Chi-town."

"Anna, that is what the Internet is for, you dummy," Rachel teased.

"Karen, you ever been there before?" Kim-1 asked.

"No, I trust my girl. That's why she's the maid of honor. She gets it done. I have no complaints at all."

"I think we're all a little tipsy," Kim-1 pointed out.

"Naw, you think so?" Anna replied.

After the round of laughter that followed, I asked Sonya and Sandra if they were having fun.

"Hey, baby girl," Sonya said, holding up her glass of wine.

"Sandra, what about you?" I asked.

"I'm okay, thank you."

"It's kind of close in here, but I think we have the right people with us, right?" I asked Sandra.

"Yeah, my future sister-in-law replied, "the others are in the other car, and Sam was left at the hotel."

I looked over at Rachel and said, "Oh, you are funny, Rachel."

"I do what I do for you," Rachel said with a grin.

"Thank you, girl!" Rachel snapped her fingers from left to right twice, a look of satisfaction on her face.

As we reached the club, I noticed that my mother and Jerry's mother had beaten us there. RTE was a new club in Chicago. But top chefs and socialites had given it great reviews. Anna looked up at the sign outside the door and asked Rachel, "What is this place like?"

"RTE is the biggest and most expensive club in the area," Rachel replied. "Celebs from Michael Jordan to Jay—Z frequently visit this club when they're in town. This was a wedding gift to Karen from a close friend in Orlando, Florida. All night, any food, drink, or entertainment is already handled for her." Rachel had known this detail, but the others hadn't. Rachel explained that Sonya E., aka Songbird, who'd had the hottest single out for the last four weeks, had provided the gift. Unable to be there for Jerry's and my big day, she'd done the next best thing—sponsored the bride's night out.

"Jerry knows her?" Anna and Tonya both asked.

"Yes, he does," Rachel replied. "He and she have been close friends for many years, and she couldn't make it, so she gave Karen this as a present. I've met her more than once, and I've always enjoyed her coming into town to visit Karen and me when she came to Atlanta. That girl loves to shop just like I do."

"I like her too," Tonya said.

As you walk into the club, you could see a huge fireplace that covered the wall on the left side of the club. Televisions in every corner showed everything from world news to local, fashion to sports. Most of the seating was along the walls. Loveseats, mainly soft, crimson red, leather sofas were arranged in the center of the room. The walls were made from Savannah brick, red in color, and added a certain touch of elegance. Lights were dim in certain places and bright in others. The bar was made of mahogany wood, and so were the stools. There were no DJs, and the music seemed to pour out from the air itself. Cuban cigars could be smelled but did not cloud the areas. Big cognac glasses were held by hands with two thousand-dollar watches around them. Toward the back were restrooms along each side of the wide hallway. Each restroom had a valet, and perfume or cologne from around the world was offered for free. Further back was the dining area.

Three-step action and soft music filled the air as well. "Mrs. J. J" was written on the banner around the VIP section. RTE had a five-star rating on its food, music, and atmosphere. This was a beautiful place for my girls and me to enjoy the night.

The music was nice and soft but loud enough that you could enjoy what was playing. I was still in a daze over Jerry being my husband soon. I also was feeling a little upset about Sam—not that we'd left her, but that Jerry had told me to let her come. He'd said that I had nothing to worry about. He'd told me to invite Leroy. That was how much he trusted me. I'd never had a man trust me that much. I sat in the VIP section and ordered a drink.

"Come *on*! Girl, you better snap out of that rotten mood," Anna said.

"Yeah, you are getting married tomorrow, and there is no one in this world going to stop that," Rachel added, pushing Karen from the side. "Now move down the seat so I can get in. This is like the movie, *The Best Man*. I am going to make sure you get over that broom." She laughed at her own joke and then looked into my eyes. "I promise you that. I would kick ass for my girl, Karen."

Everyone knew who the comment was for—Sam! But Sam wasn't there. *Where is she?* I wondered.

"Hey! You finally made it," my mother screamed. She and Mrs. Jones were out on the dance floor dancing with some young gentlemen and Sam.

"Yes, mother? I did. How long have you been here?"

The music of the SOS Band played "The Finest."

"Longer than you!" she replied.

The waitress led them back to their seats. As they sat, my mother and Jerry's mother ordered drinks and asked where the menus were.

In the back, there was an even longer bar, where there was even more room than there was in the bar area up front. The setup was both similar and different. People hung around, eating and enjoying watching others dance on the dance floor. RTE made me feel like I was in an old 1950s club and restaurant.

I looked over at Alicia. I wondered why she had that look on her face. She seemed happy, and it made me feel good to realize that my sister was glad to be here and glad that all of the people important to me were able to be here too.

"Karen, I've been taking shots of Patrón with Barbara. I like her," Alicia said.

Mrs. Watson placed a hand on Mrs. Jones shoulder, and they laughed. Sonya and Sandra were surprised to see their mother drinking. She didn't do that very often.

"Mom, you know Daddy don't want you to drink like this," I told my mother in a stern voice.

"What did you call me?" she replied. "Mom—that's right; I am your mother. You worry about Jerry. Do not worry about me. I can take care of myself, your daddy, your sisters, and you. And many other sorry children from other people around here if I have to," she added, pointing at the girls at the table.

Kim-2, who was sitting next to me, laughed.

"I want to ask you a question, Karen."

"Yes, Mother."

"Did you know that they sell chitterlings here?"

"No I did not know that."

"I'm getting some to go. Mrs. Jones, you want some?"

"No, baby," Jerry's mom replied. "I just don't eat anyone's food."

"That's what you used to tell us, Mom," Renee said, as Sam sat down next to her and Kim-1. The area was full and everyone was seated.

"Karen, are you all right?" Mrs. Jones asked.

"Yeah," I told her. "I'm just a little jumpy. That's all."

"Well, I hope you're not having second thoughts now."

"Oh no, Mrs. Jones!" I assured her. "I just have a lot on my mind."

"Well let's get something to drink and let go and have fun on the dance floor. Tomorrow, you will be just like me—Mrs. Jerry Jones. But tonight, you are a sister who is having fun with your girls!"

"Yeah, you're right." I smiled and started doing the Chicago strut away from the table to the floor.

The Kims, Anna, and I danced our way to the dance floor. All eyes were on us. We danced for at least three songs that seemed to never end.

As we came off the floor, the waiters finally came into view, carrying the drinks. There were bottles of vodka, gin, Patrón and other kinds of tequila, Chris, merlot, chardonnay, and beer. I was so out of breath I only said, "Give me a glass and my own bottle."

Imitating Shanaynay on *Martin,* someone yelled, "Take it to the head." "That's how you get your buzz on."

Laughter poured from the table, and as I took the suggestion, everybody stood up, clapping and dancing at the tables.

"That's my song," Anna said, standing on the stage by our tables. She was singing like she was Destiny's Child, "I'm a Soldier."

"I's gettin' MARRIED!" I yelled jokingly.

I sat down and started to have fun at the table with my family and friends. I could see that Sam was having a good time too. Two men were talking to her off in a corner. As the music played and the time slipped by, my entourage and I were making the best of the night in RTE. The lobster, steak, and shrimp were cooked to perfection. The service was A-one. There was never a moment when we needed anything. There even was a Michael Jordan sighting coming toward us.

"Hey, that's Michael Jordan," one of the ladies yelled out.

"Mr. Jordan, could you have a seat with me and my girlfriends?" Anna stood up and asked.

He waved and spoke to the table. Anna had a way of making any man do as she wished.

"Mr. Michael Jordan, I do declare," Mrs. Jones said with her hand out.

"Yes, Ms. . . ."

"Mrs. Jones."

"Okay, Mrs. Jones," he said, taking Jerry's mothers hand in one hand and my mother's hands in the other and shaking them both at the same time.

"My, what big hands you have," Mrs. Jones said.

"Big enough to hold me too I bet," Kim-1 added.

"Yes, I guess I could," he joked.

"But what brings you over here?" Mrs. Jones asked.

"Well I was walking around, and I saw the banner so I thought I'd stop by. Who is the young lady getting married?"

Everyone said, "Karen" and pointed in my direction.

"Hi," I said. "My fiancé wants to meet you."

"What does he do?" Mr. Jordan asked.

"He's in the clothing business," I replied. "Maybe you've heard of his line—All Me?"

"Yes, yes I have," he replied. "That's Jerry Jones, right?"

"Yes it is."

We chatted for a moment about Jerry and his line.

"Y'all gone make me lose my mind," Kim-1 cried over the DMX vocals. "I'm drunk in here. I'm drunk in here. And he is fine." Kim pointed toward Michael Jordan. "I don't want to put no Hanes on you," she said with a big grin on her face.

"Me either, sister," Anna bellowed out.

"I want to take them off." Kim-1 reached over me and tried to grab at MJ's pants.

"Hey, what are you doing?" Michael said, laughing.

"I just wanted to see if you have on Hanes underwear." Kim-1 and the ladies laughed.

If Michael was light-skinned, he would be red. He smiled and stood to his feet, as Jerry's mother, pulled Kim-1 back to her seat, saying, "Come on, baby. That man doesn't want any of you."

MJ thanked us all then said, "I think it's time for me to get back to my party up front." He looked down at me. "Karen, I wish you and your husband the best. Here is my personal card. If Jerry would really like to talk to me, I would be honored.

And from all you've said of him, you too will make it. Tell him to call me after you get back from your honeymoon."

He walked off then hesitated and returned. "Where is the honeymoon?"

"We're going to Australia for a week then to Hawaii for the final week to see the waterfalls and lovely hillsides," I replied.

"Well I trust you two will enjoy yourselves. And your last name will be again?" Michael asked, as if he had a reason.

"My last name will be Jones. We will be Mr. And Mrs. Jerry Jones," I replied.

"You mean like the Dallas Cowboys owner?" MJ smiled.

"Yes, just like that."

I thought nothing of the exchange and smiled back. Shaking his hand again, I wished him a nice evening. "Please forgive Kim-1. She's had a lot to drink."

Michael looked deeply into Karen's eyes and thought quickly to himself, *Jerry is a lucky man.* He nodded his head and disappeared in the crowd.

✳   ✳   ✳

Rachel reached over and asked me if I was she ready to leave.

"Leave?" I replied.

"Yes, we have more for you in the room. I mean your family is cool, but this section coming up is for us."

"Okay, let me tell my mom and Jerry's mother." I stood and walked over to my mother's side of the table.

"Oh, baby, that is my song." The Outkast song Bombs over Bagdah was playing, and it made all the ladies get up for one more dance.

"Mom, I'm about to leave."

My mother had joined another group of ladies who were about ten deep at another table; they were all in their fifties to seventies. "Okay, I will take care of Barbara and make sure she gets home."

"What? You need to be leaving with me," Mrs. Jones said.

"Barbara, you ready to go?" my mother asked Mrs. Jones.

"Not yet, baby! I haven't been out this late since I was in my fifties. And the men here like old women." Jerry's mother stood and started dancing with a young man near the table. This man was younger then her youngest child. She reached out to him, and he led her to the floor.

"You see. We will be all right, baby," my mom said. "Don't you do nothing wrong in that room, and don't you and that girl Sam over there get in a tussle either."

"What you mean?" I asked.

"I know what happens next. You respect yourself and your soon-to-be husband. Okay?"

"Yes, Mother."

"I will call you in the morning and make sure you are up and ready to get married, okay."

"Yes, Mother."

My mother danced away from me and the table.

"Your people having a good time? They ready to go?" Rachel asked me.

"No, they are staying, and we are going. I'm ready for another drink and some more fun. Let's get it started! I am going to be one of Hammer's girls tonight." I smiled at Rachel and motioned to the table so the girls would know it was time to leave.

As we all stood and made our way out, you could hear the laughter all the way to the front door. Everyone in the club knew there was a special party in the back. From the DJ's announcements to the flowers and balloons all around my table to the VIP rope that prohibited everyone else from entering the rear of the club, it was clear we were there for a good time. And we had a good time.

"Come on, ladies, let's rise like yeast and get out of here," Anna said, her words slurred.

All the women had been drinking and enjoying themselves to the max. I was intoxicated also, but I knew this was the time that I would have to dismiss Sam. As we reached the limos I slowed my pace and turned. "Sonya, please, girl, let the other limo drivers know that my mother and the rest of the ladies are staying, so they shouldn't leave."

"I got you girl," Sonya said as she stumbled toward the limos.

"Sam!" I cried out. "Good night!"

"What?" Sam replied.

"Look, I'm going to let you leave now without putting a kicking to your behind. I'm a bigger figure 'cause I'm a bigger nigga! Or is it that I'm a bigger nigga. Well you know what the heck I mean. So move on before you get spat on!"

"Yes, it's time you go home. You need some cab fare?" Rachel asked her.

"Hell no!" Sam snapped. "I have my own money."

Sam stood there in front of the club. *If Karen wasn't so far away I'd hit her and her sorry girlfriends*, she told herself. *But she's got her space and her buffer zone built up by silly-ass rich women.*

Even though she was very upset and very, very drunk, she knew that now was not the time to act out. If she did, she'd get stamped out. She realized that the odds were stacked against her.

The air outside was cold, and this made the tension seem to dip a little lower and colder. All I could think about was that I wanted to knock the hell out of Sam. But the distance and the people kept us apart. All the women stood around outside, waiting to see what Sam was going to say or do.

Rachel knew I wasn't going to put up with this too much longer. To my surprise, she turned toward the street and waved down a cab. Women do not like trouble like that for a friend. They'll protect their friends from anyone who may cause a problem, situation, or trouble. Anna and Rachel placed their arms under mine. To let Sam know that it was time for her to make her exit, we all turned away.

But Anna turned back and poked out her tongue once again and sang, "It's so nice that we have this time together." Anna then pointed at her behind and yelled, "Sam! Kiss this."

We all laughed again as Harry opened the door for us to fall into the limo.

I know tomorrow I will have my chance at that woman, Sam told herself as she waved down a cab. Sam was a lady—a true woman. As would any lady, she would fight for the man she loved. But fighting tonight wouldn't make much sense, as she was sure to lose. So she left proud but hurt that she had not had the chance to start, much less finish, what she'd had in mind.

There was an essence about Sam that Jerry and any other man would love. Now she was just hurt and in love; you couldn't and then you could totally fault her for how she was feeling. But she knew that tonight Karen had the upper hand.

"I need to go to 155th Street and Kedize," Sam told the driver. "I need to get me another drink." Sam stated out loud, dipping deeper into the backseat.

"Hey, you know any good clubs open tonight?" Sam asked the driver. I mean a nice club."

"Yeah I do," the driver said. "There's a place called The Crocodile Club."

"Take me there. What do they play? I mean what type of music?"

"Trust me," the driver said. "A lovely, sexy woman like you needs to be in a nice place, and the Crocodile Club is just what you need." The driver was Jamaican, and Sam found his tone pleasant.

After all that had happen tonight, Sam felt that she needed to talk. So she told her story to the driver as he drove. He didn't understand why she would have so much hatred for this lady, Karen. She should be mad at Jerry. But he continued to listen and continued to give the little advice that he could, being that he was only hearing one side of the story.

The driver offered this. "You know, back on my island, there is a saying. Would you like to hear it?"

Sam was silent, and the driver began to think she was asleep. He could smell the alcohol from her breath.

"Sorry," Sam said. "I was looking for my cell phone." She wanted to call Jerry and see if they could meet—for at least one more time. *Like Luther Vandross said, "If only for one night,"* she thought to herself. Then she remembered a poem Jerry had written. Instead of answering the driver, she told him of a night that Jerry was hurting deep inside because of a woman called Michele, how late that night he had written her a poem.

"How did it go?" The Jamaican driver asked.

There was a silence again then Sam finally remembered. "Jerry told her that most women don't believe men know when they are wrong, that they hurt the ones who mean the most to them. Jerry said that he tried to put it in his own words and to explain that he know he'd done wrong by this woman. But when the woman read it, she told him that it was worthless. She asked him why he'd awakened her to read this bull stuff."

There was a great pause in the conversation, and the driver again thought that his passenger was asleep. Then Sam blurted out, "Jerry then said, 'Sam, here is what I felt on this morning.'" She recited his poem from memory.

> *When I cry*
> *Damn she loves me, she hates me. I try to do what I know is right.*
> *The sex is gone, she don't hold me—not one night.*
> *I drink too much, hang too much,*
> *But it was this she saw when we first took flight.*
> *She loves me, she hates me. I try to do what I know is right.*
> *The drink takes my brain, makes me feel just right.*
> *I know my problems will be here after this night.*
> *I rhyme at the end of each recite*

Let me tell you how I can fight.

Verbs—action words—come from the left and . . . yeah, the right.

I fall when she leaves the room.

To God I set my sight.

They know how we are before they get us.

They know how we act before we act up.

They know we will do what we do that is not right.

But why do they love us

With all this insight!?

Damn she loves me, she hates me, and I know I'm not right.

"I like that," the driver replied. "And this is the man you want to take from this Karen woman who is getting married tomorrow?"

"Yes!" Sam replied.

"Why?"

"Well he seems to have it all together. He can write; he is funny; he can cook," Sam started.

"And he makes you fight over him with his bride," the driver interjected. "He would be a very powerful man back in my country," he joked.

Sam smiled.

The driver could see her in the rearview mirror. "That's what I was waiting for."

"What?" Sam asked.

"I wanted to see your beautiful smile. I want to tell you something. I heard my mother say it to me over and over as a child, and now I say it to my three kids."

"What's that?" Sam asked.

"She used to tell me, 'As life goes by and you are going through hell, the only way you get out of it is to keep on going.'"

"I like that," Sam said. "You're a nice man."

"Thank you," he replied. "It seems to me you feel like you're going through hell."

"I know that he loves me, and I am right," Sam replied.

"Well if he loves you so much," the driver said gently, "why is he marrying another woman?"

Sam felt really stupid. "Yeah, I wonder about that too," she admitted.

"So you need to keep on going. Don't let this be the end of a beautiful woman's life. Not one man or one woman should be the reason a person gives up on God, Jesus Christ, life, love, and family. As time goes by, you will heal, and God will bring you that special person you have been seeking. Just take each day alone as a way to better yourself for the new love God will bring too you. But once God does, you have to make sure you do not run that person away with your past or your bad habits; your bad habits should be long gone. But if you are still working on them, you need not worry. God will help you be and do your best with the next love he sends you. Our father sends us signs and messages that we are in his care—that you will be all right. And the person who hurt you last was the person God wanted you to be away from, so that you could receive your blessing from him. God puts people in our lives for a reason, a season, or a lifetime. I think that this gentleman is in your life for a reason—for you to grow.

"We as people seem to block our blessing from ourselves by staying with a person who doesn't want us," the driver continued. "God doesn't want us to do this. He doesn't want us to be unhappy. So to correct each phase in our lives, we must walk by faith and not by sight. Let go and let God guide you."

Sam listened very closely to what the driver was saying. She knew that his words were the reason she'd gotten into this cab and not another. The words this immigrant said struck Sam's heart and mind hard. She was living for the wrong reason. Sam said to herself, *I have been trying to get something that, first, isn't mine and, second, doesn't want to be mine. I need to find my own, not someone else's.* "What's your name?" Sam asked.

"Hello. My name is Amare." The driver was smiling, and Sam could see his smile in his rearview mirror.

Sam laughed a little. She remembered that Jerry use to tell her about his grandfather, Henry, who would tell him, "Get your own, not what another man has; get yours." She smiled, and tears fell, streaming onto her purse.

The driver drove into the night, watching Sam cry into her hands. The night was cold, and it seemed to keep getting colder.

Chapter Five

The Drake Hotel

I looked over the girls in the limo, smiled, and joined in the conversation. It was after midnight, and the limos pulled in front of the Drake Hotel off of Lakeshore. Chicago was beautiful at night. "Rachel, what are we doing here?"

"This is a present from me and Kim1 and 2. We are going to party and sleep here for awhile but go to change at the Hard Rock. Is that okay with you, girlfriend?"

"I guess it has to be. You better not have me looking like a rag doll today at my wedding."

"Trust me. We will have you looking beautiful."

Downtown was, as always, hustling with a steady flow of cars, people, cabs, and excitement.

"Whose name is our suite under?" Anna asked.

"It's under Karen's name," Rachel replied.

"My name!" I exclaimed. "You all trying to get me killed?"

"No!" Rachel explained. "It's Karen AM, for All Me!"

"Okay, you made me smile, you hogs."

With the wind blowing hard off of Lake Michigan and the air so cold, the ladies were ready for their party time inside.

Looking and acting intoxicated, Anna yelled out. "Hey, girl, you know we are about to act the fool up in here. Like Nelly, UP IN ERR! UP IN ERR!"

"Girl, it is up in here, not up in err," Tonya said to Anna.

"Yeah, whatever!" Anna replied. Then she turned to me. "I am so glad you let that witch have it to her face. She looked liked she was thinking, *What the heck?* I was hoping she would say something out of the ordinary so that I could put a cap in her ass."

"Anna, I think you're drunk. You don't have a gun."

"Yes I do!" Anna reached in her bag and brought out a water pistol. She started squirting the group of ladies. They all ran to get inside and away from Anna.

When the others had disappeared inside the building, Anna asked me. "Can a lady get loosey-goosey sometimes? I mean it's not like I'm getting married to a sexy black man."

"Hold up, Anna," I said. "You chose to marry Kevin. I had nothing to do with that. Anyway, we all knew you wouldn't marry a black man."

"What?" Anna said, opening the door and looking at all the girls, who were walking up to the counter. "Well, we will talk about this later, Karen." Anna rolled her eyes and stepped back, showing she was drunk. She then yelled at the counter! "Yeah, and I don't even know all these women."

"Anna, behave, no one said anything to make you act up." I said to her.

"You damn right! Rachel and Tonya said at the sametime. You better never ever call me out my name I know that. Anna said slowly . . . ."Or you will what?" Kim-2 asked her. She too spoke her mind and was the only one Anna was going to listen to that night.

"I never!"

"You never what?"

"Never seen a dick I didn't like," Anna slurred out.

Some of the ladies laughed, and the other just didn't know what to think or say.

"Kim-2, please get this girl and take her by the elevators," I said. I had hoped this wouldn't happen. But as we all know, when you mix drinking with old friends, someone's going to do something crazy.

Anna turned to Rachel. "Don't think we didn't see you in his car," she blurted out. "Lord only knows why your head was moving and nothing else."

"Anna, what are you talking about?"

"Rachel, I saw you by the football field.

"Oh, please. Let's get her behind up stairs," Rachel said. "Can we have our keys?"

"Ladies, are you guests here at the Drake Hotel?" The desk man asked, as Anna was getting louder and louder.

"And another thing," she started.

"Anna, cool out. Let's take this upstairs," Tonya said to her.

"Anna, don't you say a thing," Rachel yelled back at her from the counter.

I had to compose myself and make a quick response to the gentlemen. "Yes, Karen Am, please."

"Okay," the man responded, finding the reservation. "You have adjoining suites on the Presidential floor. Do you have any bags?"

"Yes, I told him. They're in the limo outside. And later, I'm expecting guests."

"Of the male kind!" Rachel added.

The clerk handed the keys to Karen.

"HEEEYYYY!" Anna yelled out, addressing strangers in the lobby, "You coming to the party?"

An older white couple walking by to the elevators looked at Anna. The woman mumbled, "Oh my goodness."

"You can take this one. I was holding it for us," Kim-1 said to the couple.

Kim-1 and 2 grabbed Anna by the arms and turned her toward the wall facing the corner.

The lobby was not crowded, but it had action going from one side to the other. People were not looking, or worrying about anyone else but themselves. With all the attention and the yelling the girls where giving each other, you could say they were the only ones paying themselves any mind at all. This was the Drake, but it was also Chicago.

Seeing what I was dealing with, Alicia and Renee came in from the lounge. "Anna, cool out. This is a special day. Keep your little-girl attitudes in check for at least forty-eight hours. You have all your life to hate each other. Do not bring that mess in here! Okay?" Renee said.

"Yeah, whatever. I will finish this stuff up stairs," Anna stated. "And like I care! You don't scare me." Anna turned around from the wall and pushed out her chest as if to say come and get some.

"Renee!" Kim-1 cut in. "I am chill, for now."

"But you better get your girl, Renee said.

Anna made a quick turn and walked toward the elevators. The doors opened like she had known they would for her. Anna walked in, followed by the Kims.

"And I will always be a *laddddyyyy*," Anna snapped back as she tried her best to walk upright while closing her fur around her body."

"Karen, you okay?" Alicia asked.

"Yeah," I said. "I'm just enjoying the show. Let them go at it for all I care. I want to party. You know Anna's ass will be asleep soon, and Rachel, well, she's probably going to get her freak on."

"But doesn't she have a man?" Tonya asked.

"You know when the cat's away, THE PUSSYCAT WILL PLAAAYYYY!" Anna yelled, as Kim-2 pushed her into the elevator wall.

The girls laughed at Anna and they all got into the elevator. We all exited the elevator and walked to the room door, as Rachel grabbed for the door handle, the door opened and there was one of the most hamsome men I have seen before in my life. He was all of six feet seven inches no shirt on and speedo swim trunks. His muscles remind me of those Playgirl men in the magazines. There was music playing behind him and more men dancing all half nake. Well Karen you said you wanted to have a traditional party! Here it is! Tonya said as she and the others started screaming and walking in pass me with their hands up in the air. I walked in and was greeted with an English model chair with a high back and two men with nothing at all on. I sat Rachel closed the door and . . . .

From Beginning to the End

Their Backs Agianst the Wall Vol 2.

Puerto Rico

In the room, I was thinking back to the days when Jerry and I had traveled together. My mind flashed back to a morning that was so beautiful.

I sat next to Jerry and said, "Honey, wake up."

"Please fasten your seatbelts. We will be touching down in about five minutes," the flight attendant said over the intercom.

"Huh! Are we there yet?"

"The sun is out, and I feel like kissing you all over your body." My eyes sank into Jerry's half-open brown eyes. "Baby, wake up. I want you to see the beach."

"Okay, I'm up," Jerry replied. "We're there already, huh."

"Yes! I am so excited. This is my first time in Puerto Rico. I hope your friend is at the airport."

"Karen, he said he would be there. I can always count on him."